The Dark Side of the Moon

Adventures in Sci-Fi, Fantasy & Horror

Jose Rodriguez

The Dork Side of the Moon
Adventures in Sci-Fi, Fantasy & Horror

v2.0

Outskirts Press, Inc.
http://www.outskirtspress.com

ISBN: 978-1-4787-8900-0

PRINTED IN THE UNITED STATES OF AMERICA

Acknowledgements

Authors—Stephen King, Neil Gaiman, Anne Rice, Charles deLint, Bentley Little, Christopher Moore, H.P. Lovecraft, John Connolly, James O'Barr, Sandra Cisneros, Isabel Allende, Joe Hill, C.S. Lewis, J.R.R. Tolkien, Edgar Allen Poe and George R. R. Martin

Lisa Moreno—because in the End, you were my very last Muse

Alyce—some bonds don't require blood ties

Fernando—for gifting me with Daenarys on my Name Day

Victor, Lilia and Marc—for checking up on me on April 21, 2016, my Darkest Day

Above all else, these stories are dedicated to my two greatest inspirations—Prince Rogers Nelson and Sonia Salazar, who, as Fate would have it, both left my world on the very same day.

Lastly, to Death herself....NotYet

A
Author's Disclaimer

Please be advised that my writing is what could be called an "acquired taste." Some of the subject matter may not apply to you; some may very well offend you. But, if you get nothing else from this reading experience, at least learn this: most of what we read and hear and see daily is made up of lies. Sometimes, even when it's packaged and sold to you as fiction, you can find Truth.

"I'm making stuff up, but I will tell you true things."

-Neil Gaiman

Contents

The Dork Side of the Moon

The Dark Side of the Moon—Secret Underground Alien Base

The Imperial Hozer paced back and forth across the conference room. Turning to face his second-in-command, General Furnee, he bellowed, "I alone am the Military Head of the Q'lero people! Why should I listen to any of you?"

"With all due respect, sir, no one, least of all myself, is questioning your authority in any way, shape or form. I merely suggested that prior to your planned invasion of this so-called Earth, it might be advisable to send a scouting mission," General Furnee calmly answered.

"You are not assigned to advise me, Furnee. You are merely to follow the orders I alone choose to give! When I want your opinion, I'll give you one!" the Imperial Hozer roared.

"Of course, sir. However, let me point out one final thing. Of all the races in all the galaxies we've enslaved so far, these Earthlings are the only ones to have attained capacity to traverse space. As such, I feel compelled to repeat my advice about sending a scout to better prepare our assault."

Finally accepting his right-hand-man's logic, Hozer shrugged his shoulders. "Very well, but I am not wasting any of our elite troops! Send my idiot brother-in-law for this menial task!"

Somewhere in the middle of the San Gabriel Valley...

D'Yego looked around the street corner to which his transporter beam had sent him. Having sent an unmanned spy pod ahead, he knew how to dress to fit in, or at least not to stand out. Aside from being entirely hairless, his people could pass as humans.

General Furnee had told him this was an important mission that must not be fouled up as was his past history. His order were clear—Find out as much as possible about the Earthlings by finding either a library or bookstore, absorb the materials into his Accumulator, then speed-read through it all back at the Mothership before writing up his report.

D'Yego surveyed his surroundings, noticing the primitive dwellings and the vehicles, which still rode on the ground. He had to wonder how these people ever achieved space travel.

After walking only two city blocks, D'Yego stopped, not believing his luck. On the next corner stood his objective—Gary's Corner Bookstore. Finding the front door locked, D'Yego pressed the Dematerializer button on his utility belt and, a second later, he was inside the building.

Aboard the Mothership, beside the Moon, inside D'Yego's private Quarters

D'Yego leafed through the thin multi-colored books in fascination. His race had the power to absorb knowledge by simply touching books or any written matter, but the human archives were unlike anything he had ever studied.

The more D'Yego kept reading however, the more he became convinced that it would be a mistake to go forward with the planned attack.

These humans had faced alien invasion many times in their past. Though technologically Earth was at least ten generations behind Q'lero, they had something extra. Apparently, there were dozens of super-powered beings on Earth whose sole purpose was to defend its citizens against any and all threats. As such, they were advanced scientifically, but put to the test in hand-to-hand combat; even a toddler on Earth would best them.

Because of all these things, D'Yego knew he must recommend that the attack on Earth be avoided at all costs. Just one or two of Earth's heroes would be enough not only to stop them, but possibly decimate the entire fleet with ease.

And yet, besides the fear he felt, D'Yego could not help but be impressed with the tales of the selflessness of Earth's protectors. Time and again, according to chronicles, not only did many risk their lives to help the powerless, some actually went as far as to willingly sacrifice themselves. All this and more he resolved to include in his report.

Hours later...

"Balderdash! This report is rubbish! It's complete and utter nonsense! These humans have never ventured outside their own solar system, and you have the stones to tell me that they pose a threat...to us?" the Imperial Hozer growled at D'Yego.

"With all due respect that is due to you, oh-very-great-one," D'Yego whimpered, "technologically, they are eons behind us, that is without dispute. However, as I included in that paper, um, now being crumbled in your hand and um, tossed at my head, these humans have living among them super-powered individuals and some groups whose sole purpose is to protect the merely mortal."

"Mutants?" General Furnee asked, obviously very interested.

"Some of them, sir, were born mutated, yes, but most acquired their powers or abilities in different ways. Let's see," D'Yego quickly recalled his readings. "Some by radiation, others by scientific experimentation, and some constructed special suits and one, I believe their most powerful protector, is actually an alien himself, but was raised as a human."

"From what planet does he originate?" General Furnee asked anxiously.

D'Yego gulped nervously before answering, "From Krypton, Sir."

Stunned looks appeared on the faces of the other commanders, while General Furnee's appearance grew even more serious. The Imperial Hozer's expression turned from one of anger to disgust at his crew's visible dismay.

"Fools!" he bellowed. "Krypton is a myth that surely the humans have heard of and created a work of fiction, as we do on our home planet when we hear of other worlds and their fables and legends! I remain unconvinced and so at this time tomorrow, when I give my signal, our attack will commence just as was originally planned."

The crew was dismissed pending further orders, but General Furnee gestured to D'Yego to follow him to his own quarters.

Moments later...

D'Yego sped back to San Gabriel in an escape pod General Furnee had provided. It would not be noticed while another ride on the transporter beam would have alerted their main computer.

General Furnee was no coward, but he cared more about his crew's safety than the galactic glory craved by the Imperial Hozer. As a result, he had re-sent D'Yego to Earth to plead for mercy if the attack couldn't be fully avoided.

The pod landed in a vacant lot about a block from the ransacked bookstore. Donning his 'human-like' attire, D'Yego walked back to the scene of his recent crime.

Meanwhile, nearby, from the opposite direction, but at about the same time...

The four teenage friends strode purposefully toward their favorite hangout—Gary's comic shop. Alyce, a huge Harry Potter fan, collected Doctor Strange issues; Chris loved Batman and Spiderman; Dennis liked the Flash and Green Lantern; and Joy preferred the Hulk and his cousin She-Hulk. They all stopped dead in their tracks when they read the bold print on the front door to Gary's—'Closed Due to Robbery.' Stunned, the four youths alternated staring mutely at the sign then at each other.

Finally, Chris, a devout Catholic, spoke up, "This is sacrilegious! Almost like stealing gold from a church!"

Dennis nodded in agreement, adding, "This is soooo against the Jedi Code!"

"This is pure, unadulterated bullshit!" Joy yelled, much to her companions' surprise, since she seldom raised her voice, much less to use profanity. Only Alyce remained quiet, her anger barely kept in check.

D'Yego was only meters from the four friends, and his blood ran even colder than normal. He felt his mission might be even easier than expected, as these youths looked exactly like the super-beings in the books. To normal, everyday citizens, they seemed to be what was termed nerds, dorks or dweebs, but in truth, that was just a secret identity to protect themselves and their loved ones. Gathering up all his courage, D'Yego timidly walked over to the youths and, in a halting, nervous voice, he began.

"Greetings, Earthlings. I come in peace with an urgent message that may save the lives of both your people and mine."

Holding several issues of assorted comic books tightly to his chest, D'Yego related all of Imperial Hozer's plans, his own discoveries regarding Earth's heroes and General Furnee's wish to stop the attack.

After revealing every last detail, D'Yego still felt his audience needed more evidence to convince them. Once they were allowed to inspect his vessel, he knew they would believe.

"This is some serious X-Files type of shit!" Alyce said, breaking her self-imposed silence.

"So, will you help us avoid war?" D'Yego almost pleaded.

"You want us to do what exactly?" Dennis inquired.

"Come back to the Mothership with me, make a display of your powers and convince my leader not to attack at all!"

"Uh...one minute please," Dennis managed before looking over at his comrades and declaring, "Group Huddle Time!"

"I think Deeyaygo believes us to be superheroes, like in the comics he assumed were based on true stories of Earth!" Dennis stated.

"Wow, was that evident to you, too, Captain Obvious?" his sister Joy said with some disdain.

"Relax, Wonder Twins!" Chris demanded. "I think it's time we put our science projects to good use, especially since our fellow humans rely on our next move!"

"You bet your ass!" Alyce agreed, shouting in agreement.

Dennis walked back to the eager alien. "Give us a few minutes to don our costumes, and we'll go with you!"

Back onboard the Mothership, after a heated discussion between General Furnee and Imperial Hozer

"This sounds like insubordination with a hint of treason, Furnee! But, I'll see your co-called Ambassadors from Earth, and then, perhaps, I'll have you executed beside them!"

D'Yego led in the youths-- Chris, Dennis, Joy were dressed in red, white and blue Haz-Mat suits, respectively. Alyce was clad in a floor-length black velvet gown complete with a hood covering most of her face. They had agreed in advance to be brief and to the point in name and showmanship.

Chris stepped forward first, trying not to be intimidated by several dozen troops surrounding the Imperial Hozer and General Furnee. "I am Fly-Boy!" he called out, triggering his hidden jet pack and soaring over the stunned crowd, before landing a tad clumsily beside his pals.

"I am known as the Whiz Kid!" Dennis yelled. Then his high-tech sneakers sped him a super-human speed through and around the amazed crowd.

"I am Super Chick!" Joy hollered, holding up two steel weights, each marked 500 pounds. "Each of these weights five times as much as your average Q'lero! Come try to lift them your puny selves!" she dared.

The Imperial Hozer eyed one of his guards, who obediently went to try his strength. By then, Joy had set them back down and flipped a hidden switch causing magnets to activate, rendering the weights essentially unmovable.

Next it was Alyce's turn. "Greetings and fair warning people of Q'lero! You will now witness the almost-limitless power of Davina, Daughter of the Dark Arts, Mistress of the Mystic, Queen of the Crypts, Knower of the Gnostic..."

Chris, Dennis, and Joy rolled their eyes, shook their head and slapped their face, respectively, as Alyce went on with self-imposed titles for another five minutes.

The arrogance was quickly forgotten as her own 'power' went on display. Alyce used smoke bombs, flash grenades and other assorted homemade fireworks to prove her point. She smiled, almost unseen, as she saw most of the troops moving slowly toward the other side of the room.

"Bah! Enough of these parlor tricks! Execute these Earthlings as well as General Furnee and my worthless turd of a brother-in-law!" Imperial Hozer roared.

"I don't think so!" Furnee replied to Hozer's bewilderment. "The troops are under my command now, Hozer. Your plans for Earth have been aborted by my decree!"

"Apparently, General Furnee also convinced others of the futility in attacking Earth!" D'Yego whispered to his Earthling friends what they had already guessed.

As the no-longer-Imperial Hozer was detained, unarmed, and led to a detention cell, D'Yego asked the four teens, "How can we repay your invaluable kindness?"

"Our reward is that justice has been done!" Dennis yelled before receiving Joy's elbow in the gut.

"Seriously though," she added, "two things—one, return to our planet only under peaceful circumstances, and two, replace all the items your stole from our, um…library!"

"It shall be so!" D'Yego cried joyfully adding, "After I make copies of these marvelous tales, of course!"

Days Later...

Chris was on the phone with his Uncle Joe, a semi-famous Hollywood screenwriter. He told him everything they had seen and done and breathlessly awaited Joe's reaction.

"Sounds like Galaxy Quests meets The Three Amigos with a bonus Witch thrown into the mix! You need a little more originality if you want to be as successful as me, kid!"

Chris did a double-take, staring off at his imaginary audience.

Bobo

Siberia, Late 1800's

Nikka sat under the huge oak, hugging her toy bear tightly to her chest, her scraped little knees nearly at her face. She brushed away the flow of tears with one of her bruised arms. When that didn't stop them, she turned her head into the bark and allowed herself to cry.

Nikka thought about trying to run away again, but then knew it was pointless. Twice before she'd tried, but the little cabin she lived in was surrounded by a deep forest. The further one ventured in, the darker it got. The tree branches actually managed to blot out the sky's light once you had walked far enough.

The first time, she'd gotten too scared to go farther than a mile or so and had turned back. Last time, she had gone further but had run into a pack of wolves. Had her father not come by with his rifle, she would surely have died. Only, looking back know, Nikka had thought that might have been the better way out.

She considered a third attempt into the mysterious woods because she couldn't even think about returning to him. Up until last night, it had been mostly yelling with the occasional back handed slap. But after her evening bath, he had crossed the line. No, she thought, there was no way she could go back. She'd rather take her chances with the wolves.

Nikka held up her bear with both hands and stared into his one good glass eye. "I wish you could help me, Bobo. I wish you could make him stop hurting me."

"Maybe he can."

Nikka looked to her right, shocked to see anyone else in what was supposed to be an uninhabited forest. It was another little girl, about her age, wearing a dark purple dress and long black hair, much of which covered most of her face. Nikka could tell she had large eyes, like a deer almost, but the beauty of them was eclipsed by her mouth, which, while normal-looking, was painted in what seemed like black lipstick.

"Don't be afraid," the strange little girl said. "I won't hurt you. I'm here to help you."

"Who are you?" Nikka asked, still fiercely clutching her bear.

"Call me Sam," she answered shyly. "I'm here to make your wish come true!"

"What wish?" asked Nikka, knowing full well what Sam referred to.

Sam's expression turned from friendly to dead serious in an instant, and then she replied, "I can make sure he never touches you again."

"Ever?" Nikka asked timidly.

"Never again. I just need your permission to do what must be done."

"Okay," Nikka said, already feeling her living nightmare was at an end.

"Splendid!" Sam almost shouted, clapping her hands together, her grin showing off what looked like sharp teeth.

Sam put out her hand, which Nikka hesitantly took, and swiftly jabbed a needle into Nikka's pinky. Nikka instinctively tried to pull her hand back, but Sam held it until the first drop of blood plopped directly onto Bobo's good eye.

"Now you must return home," Sam told Nikka.

"I thought it was all over," Nikka almost sobbed.

"Not until you go to him...then Bobo can help you end it."

"Alright," Nikka said, head turned down.

Holding her bear in one hand, Nikka took the outstretched arm offered by Sam and let herself be helped to her feet. Sam pointed back the way she came, and Nikka reluctantly began her journey home.

An hour later, Nikka and Bobo arrived at the cabin, where her father was waiting outside, belt at his side.

Nikka kept walking toward him, hugging Bobo against her chest. As the first lash came down, she turned swiftly, so the blow came down across her back, leaving her companion unharmed.

"How dare you worry me, you ungrateful, little brat!" her father shouted.

Annoyed at her defensive crouch, he snatched away her bear, flinging it over his shoulder, into the open doorway of the cabin.

Nikka started to cry out a protest only to be abruptly silenced by a backhand to the mouth. The force of the blow knocked her to the ground. She struggled to get back to her feet, only to have a boot push her back down.

Nikka looked up at her father standing menacingly over her, tears and snot mixing with the blood trickling from her lips. She looked around for her bear only to be slapped again.

They both heard the noise from inside the cabin. It was a low growl that quickly became a roar.

Nikka's father turned in time to see a grizzly emerge from the doorway. Rearing on its hind legs, the creature looked at least ten feet tall. Paralyzed with fear, he did nothing as the bear's front paw swatted him to the ground.

Nikka watched in horror as her bear ambled over calmly to her screaming father, opened its mouth and tore out his throat.

Though she had imagined her toy would magically come to life, seeing her dark fantasy play out was still too much for her to handle. Steeling her nerves, Nikka scrambled to her feet and raced back into the darkening woods.

Before disappearing into the trees, Nikka thought she heard a rough voice cry out, "Wait!"

She lost a shoe and the little apron on the front of her dress but didn't stop running until the light ran out, and she lowered her pace to avoid tripping on a root or smacking into a low branch.

Nikka walked on until she noticed the pain from the bottoms of her feet. She sat to inspect them as best she could and felt what she suspected was blood on her soles. From nearby, there came the sound of voices, and Nikka stayed as still as possible in order to listen.

One voice she recognized as that of the girl Sam, and she was saying, "What do you mean I can't have her?!?"

Another little girl's voice answered, in a sweet, almost melodious tone, "She doesn't belong to you because she is unaware of the choice between good and evil. She is innocent and merely sought to end her suffering. As such, she belongs to us."

Sam answered, much angrier now, "She knew what her bear would do!"

"She wished it would stop her pain, but she had no real concept of death! You witnessed how she reacted to his demise! It was fear and regret, not the joy and relief of those truly evil. You have no claim on her."

"Well then, damn you, but most of all, damn Him!" Sam yelled.

Then there was an explosion followed soon after by the smell of sulfur.

A moment later, Nikka heard footsteps, and she looked up to see the approach of Sam's conversation partner. This little girl was literally glowing and, where Sam had made her feel nervous and slightly uncomfortable, the new visitor brought with her only a sense of peace and calm she had never experienced before in her short life.

"It's all right, Nikka," she said. "I won't hurt you."

"Who are you?" Nikka managed.

"You can call me Micaela. I'm going to take you home to our real father."

"Really?!?" Nikka almost cried tears of joy with the sudden knowledge that her nightmare life was at an end. Whatever lay beyond had to be better.

Micaela put out her hand, which Nikka took without hesitation. An instant later, Nikka's rags were replaced with a beautiful white dress to match her new friend. They began to walk onto an invisible set of stairs when Nikka once again heard a rough voice call out, "Wait!"

Nikka and Micaela turned to see the approach of what had been a toy and was now an enormous killing machine.

Micaela's glow even helped illuminate the fact that Bobo's glass eye was now replaced by a very real, tearful one.

The bear sat back on its hind legs and, with its front paws in a prayer-like gesture, cried, "Please, take Bobo with you! Me no eat nobody no more!"

Nikka's face turned back to Micaela with a pleading look.

Micaela only smiled and said, "Very well."

Nikka squealed with delight and went to hug Bobo, who had to have his nose blown after his own blubbering subsided.

Climbing on Bobo's back, Nikka followed Micaela back up the unseen steps. She had the first grin her face had ever known. Nikka was going home. And so was Bobo.

TWO BROTHERS -a children's story

Introduction

There is a belief held by Jehovah's Witnesses that is coincidentally shared by some obscure Mormon texts. That is the theory that Jesus Christ and the Archangel Michael are one and the same being.

Satan was once one of the Archangels, in fact, one of the seven who are allowed to see the very Face of God. Add to that the Biblical fact that Angels are also known as "Sons of God."

Taking all that into account, I created my own semi-heretical 'What If?' scenario—For if Jesus and the Devil actually began their existence as brothers, then all of human history, religiously-speaking, has been one long case of sibling rivalry—the Good son versus the Rebellious Youth, so to speak.

That will be the premise of this short story, written almost as a type of adult-oriented children's story. It will begin slightly before the Creation, go through the Biblical encounters between the 'brothers' and end, fittingly, I think, at the Book of Revelations.

Once upon a time, there was a Time Before. Only God existed then, only He and nothing more.

Can you imagine? There was no Earth and no Sea, no one like you or me. There were no elephants or flowers. There was only God and His Everlasting Power.

But all this emptiness made God lonely and maybe a little bit bored. After all, there was no one around to know that He was the Lord.

First, He created Heaven to have a place to call Home. Indeed, it was heavenly sitting on the very first throne.

Next, God created His children. Angels were the very first race. Only the Original Seven would ever look upon His face.

There was Sammael, Michael, and Gabriel, followed by Raphael and Uriel and then Jophiel and Israfel. This was long before the creation of Hell.

Those Seven were the first batch and so, the Most Beloved. A little later, scores more were made in that Kingdom up above.

Content with his children, God focused on filling the sky. The Sun, stars and Moon were made to fill the void up high.

Then God made the Earth: the Flora, Fauna and Man. He did it all with a Word and the wave of His hand.

All of the Angels were told to bow before this Adam that day. And all did as they were told, except Sammael, who asked, "Why should a Son of Fire bow to a Son of Clay?"

This opinion spread quickly and rebellion was born. Soon, a third of the Angels sided with the 'Star of the Morn.'

Michael chose to lead those loyal to the Most High. War erupted in Heaven, and the first tears ever were cried.

Michael and Sammael had been the closest brothers of all. That friendly bond was broken the Day of the Fall.

Michael was forced to cast down the very Blood of his Blood. Sammael, who had known Glory, slammed into a puddle of mud.

Cleaning the muck off, Sammael shook his fist at the sky. "No longer am I your servant! I will become the Father of Lies!"

He changed his name to Devil and Satan, both of which mean only Adversary. Since he knew all of God's laws, he vowed to do their contrary.

Satan set his eyes on Adam and deceived him through his wife. Listening to him cost them Paradise and forever changed their life.

For generations afterward, Satan continued tricking the race of Man. He hurt God in this way, as it disrupted the Master Plan.

But God had already decided to send Michael to show the Way. He would reclaim His flock, who, like sheep, had just gone astray.

With but a Word, God made a virgin heavy with child. The greatest weapon against Satan would be a baby, meek and mild.

Michael was raised as human, with the joy and fear of any child. But before his mission began, he would face Satan alone in the wild.

Some thirty years along, in the desert they met. Satan had no idea who he really faced, at least not yet.

He assumed that this 'Jesus' was some sort of prophet, not a king. Nothing good came from Nazareth, not a single, solitary thing.

Satan offered the usual temptations up to and including the world entire. When all these were refused, Satan guessed this Son of Clay had formerly been a Son of Fire.

Satan bided his time, while Jesus went on to preach the Word. He would devise a plan so the Message went unheard.

Satan watched as Jesus fed the hungry and healed the sick. He felt time was short as he heard the Eternal Clock tick.

Satan focused on the Twelve, those Jesus called to be his own. He picked out one in particular, who was discontent following a king with no throne.

Satan thought he had won with the ease of Judas' betrayal. He was unaware God's Master Plan had always involved a cross and three nails.

How the Devil laughed as Jesus hung from that tree. He was unaware Mankind's fate depended on this Son's agony.

Satan's rejoicing was short-lived, and the joy became gloom a mere three days later when his brother emerged from the tomb.

Satan's rage grew and directed itself on Michael's growing followers instead. He vowed to see them all dead.

He turned them against each other, but when their numbers only grew, he convinced them to make war, especially on the Muslim and Jews.

More than two thousand years passed and much blood was shed. There came a time when the living grew to envy the dead.

Michael returned, no longer a sacrificial lamb, but with the roar of a lion.

Leading his army once more, Michael chained up his brother foot and hand. Sammael was tossed into a bottomless Abyss to nevermore roam freely on our land.

Michael became King, ruling over the Faithful who remained. Gone were all the evils that had caused our souls to stain.

There were no more tears and vanquished was all sorrow and pain. But we remembered the cost of victory so we would never fall again.

But wait! What of Sammael, the errant brother and wayward son? Though he had been defeated, his story was not yet done.

Tumbling into his new prison, Sammael gave not a backwards glance. He did not realize his Father was about to offer a second chance.

Inside his head, Sammael heard words and learned the meaning of Mercy. If he would only repent, he could return to the Silver City.

But Sammael's millennia-old anger had given him a false sense of pride. It prevented him from revealing what he truly felt inside.

Instead he declined forgiveness for things he claimed not to regret. And though he had been banished, he claimed not to be beaten yet.

And to this very day, Sammael plunges further from the Eyes of Man. But, if our hearts ever falter, he may re-emerge and victorious stand.

The End?

Pancho Villa's Last Ride

"You know, Pancho Villa, wasn't the Robin Hood you think he was," my father told me one day, while I was watching an old film on the Mexican Revolution of 1910.

I never really presumed that, you know? From my constant reading, I've come to find that most historical figures are neither the saints their fans claim nor the sinners their dictators would have us believe. However, the idealists I've ended up admiring, those who have tried to help their fellow man (i.e. Kennedys and Martin Luther King, Jr.) always end up with a bullet in their head. I had put Villa in that category, but since I knew my father was not given to one-sentence commentaries, I lowered the volume and turned to listen.

"In the summer of 1965, I worked as a ranch hand in Chihuahua for a cattle baron named Jose Luis Terrazas. Around the campfire one night, I commented to our supervisor how it was a coincidence our boss had the same name as the Hacienda owner who years ago had tried to rape Pancho Villa's sister, resulting in a shooting and the beginning of Villa's career as a bandit."

"It's no coincidence," the rancher answered somberly. "The Patron is that man's son."

Seeing my jaw drop, he added something even more surprising.

"And that's nothing. In 1923, the Jefe was one of the men who conspired against the late General Villa. It is said he may have been one of the men who actually fired the shots that ended the revolutionary hero's life."

"How can you work for such a man? A traitor to our very country!" I exclaimed.

"It was all before my time," he said with a shrug. "Besides, I have a family to feed. When you have one of your own, trust me, you'll be kissing the gringos' asses to put food in your kid's mouths."

"That comment shut me up, but I kept the story in mind. I was only hired for that summer, so when I went to collect my last pay, I asked to see Mr. Terrazas. The foreman looked at me strangely, but went to ask if the Patron would allow me a visit. To his surprise, it was approved and, hat in hand, I was escorted into the main house."

"Flanked by two armed bodyguards, Jose Luis Terrazas II sat in a high-backed chair, a blanket covering his legs. The old man, who had to be in his late seventies or early eighties, had a cigar in one hand and a tumbler of Brandy in the other."

Eyeing me curiously, he asked gruffly, "Was the pay too little for you?"

"No sir," I replied somewhat intimidated by the guards. "I was hoping you could tell me about the assassination of General Francisco Villa."

"At first, Terrazas looked startled to hear the name, but, just as suddenly, his face took on a more distant look as his memories flew back across the years."

"Ah yes, Doroteo Arango," he said using Villa's original name in an almost derogatory way. "It's been a long time since anyone brought that up, at least in front of me. You have cojones, boy, so I will indulge your curiosity."

"Let me begin with the fact that my father inadvertently set off Villa on his destiny. But I must explain…back then, it was tradition for the Hacienda owner, or his oldest son, to partake in the marriage bed of any peon's daughter before her husband. Arrango's sister resisted, as many did, and her brother broke tradition by interfering. He shot my father several times, but did not succeed in killing him. A fatal mistake, you see, for years later, my father made me swear to avenge this trespass on his person. Being a man of honor, I, of course, agreed. Only by this time, Arango was Pancho Villa and a hero to the common people, but never to the legitimate government."

"By the end of our bloody Revolution, I was heir to my father's land and money. I used that to influence other like-minded individuals to join a plot I was forming. I falsely claimed that Villa would come out of retirement and seek public office, effectively ensuring their support. No one with any kind of power or property wanted that, you see."

"Once the conspirators were set, the rest came easily. We bought an abandoned building in a park Villa was known to drive by frequently, and we waited. Twice we were thwarted; once by a flock of pigeons, another by a crowd of schoolchildren blocking our view. An overzealous member of our group vowed that Villa would not escape a third attempt, kids or no kids, he would shoot. Fortunately, no one was between us and our target on July 20, 1923. We opened the windows and fired until our guns were empty. Something neither history books nor movies reveal is that Villa, ripped apart by bullets already, reached across his torn belly and pulled out his pistol, firing at an idiot who had been too eager and had run out to fire at the revolutionary."

With that said Terrazas let out a cough-filled laugh and uncovered his legs. "The idiot never walked again!"

My father took a swig of his can of Bud Lite and continued.

"Two years later, I was working in Oregon alongside your uncles picking pears. It was long hours and little pay, most of which we sent back to Jalpa to help your grandparents. On our day off, there wasn't really much to do, as we were far from any big towns."

"Some of us wasted our leisure time drinking, myself included. I make no apologies. It has always been a weakness of mine. Well, that and women, but those are altogether different stories."

"Regardless, one Saturday evening, after our labors were done and we were relaxing after some cold showers, your Uncle Ruben brought up a rumor he'd overheard. It seemed that nearby to our worksite there lived and old hermit-like American World War I veteran, who had, in his youth, fought Villa's troops."

(In March of 1916, Villa was accused of raiding Columbus, New Mexico and killing civilians. It was the only foreign attack on American soil in the 20th century until Pearl Harbor. Villa, however, continued to deny his involvement in the Columbus incident until his death. Villa may have been many things, but a liar wasn't one of those he was known for.)

"Being bored out of our minds," my father continued, "we resolved to seek out this veteran the following day and see if he would amuse us with a story of Villa."

"The old soldier's cabin deep in the Oregon woods was surprisingly easy to find, and we took a gift of Jack Daniels whiskey to soften our meeting. Since your Uncle Ruben had been in this country longer and knew far more English, I let him do all of the talking."

"It took several knocks on the door before he answered, and, even then, he only opened it a small crack. But after my brother gave the old man a friendly hello and showed him the bottle, his eyes brightened, and he let us in."

"After we'd all had a shot and my brother had revealed the reason for our visit, the crusty old-timer lit a pipe, leaned back in his rocking chair and agreed to humor us."

"Yep" he began, "I was part of the so-called Punitive Expeditionary Campaign led by General 'Black Jack' Pershing outta Fort Bliss. I had trained under Patton back when he was just a Lieutenant. Quite a temper that Patton, but always a patriot and a good soldier."

"Anyhow, what we ended up doing would today most likely be seen as a violation of International Law. You know, going into a sovereign nation without a declaration of war or heck, not even asking permission. But we were soldiers, sworn to protect our country, which had been attacked. Villa was to be captured, dead or alive."

"It was the first time Americans used airplanes for war. The job of the1st Aero Squadron was only to observe location and movement of the enemy. Uncle Sam sent 600 planes south with us, and they all returned. Well, all but one. Some Mexican child stole one right in the middle of the campaign and shot up our campground, tearin' up our tents and spookin' our horses. None of the troops was even scratched, but the ignorant bastard crashed the plane and got hisself killed before we had a chance to knock him outta the sky."

"The Mexicans put that incident into one of their ballads. Of course, since we never made any mention of it, it might as well never have happened! He-he. Anyhow, besides them planes, we were 10,000 strong. Even with that kind of man power, lookin' for Villa across Chihuahua was like that sayin' about the needle in the haystack. Some of us figured Villa was bein' cowardly, not darin' to face our superior military might. What our Intel revealed later was that around the time of our so-called invasion, Villa had been wounded by Federales during a battle near Parral."

"What little information we could gather from the reluctant campesinos was basically the same—Villa had a bad leg wound and was hiding out in a cave somewhere in the hills. That's about the time our Lieutenant Patton, frustrated for lack of action, decided to go against any target he could find. Soon enough he got his chance. We heard that close by our encampment, General Julio Cardenas was holed up in some friend's home, awaiting orders. Cardenas was Captain of Villa's elite troops, the Dorados, and also one of his personal bodyguards."

"Now up 'til then, we had been marchin' on foot ridin' horseback, but Patton had the idea to get the jump on Cardenas by using the few Dodges we had with us. That was the first time combat involved a moving vehicle, by the way."

"We drove through the little pueblo called Tomochic, inhabited mostly by unfriendly Tarahumara Indians. Not even Spaniards had broken those savages. We surrounded the hut and our Lieutenant called out, in the little Spanish he had picked up, for the Villistas to surrender or else. To his credit, Cardenas ran out, guns a'blazin', and Patton was forced to shoot him dead. Several others ran out also, and one got away on a nearby horse. The rest met Cardenas' fate. Patton had us tie the dead General to his Dodge's hood, like a deer, and we drove back to camp that way."

"Needless to say, the troops' morale improved considerably after that. The Lieutenant began sending us out in squads of ten, hoping that the killing of Cardenas would force other Villistas out of hiding. Although our mini-campaign had succeeded, we hadn't retrieved any info on Villa's whereabouts, bein' that we had to shoot all the possible witnesses. Heh-heh!

Anyhow, a week later, I was among a group of ten under a Major Tompkins, I believe it was. We were explorin' an area a few miles south of Tomochic when alluva sudden, we was surrounded. And I mean totally all around screwed! There were about a hundred armed horsemen led by General Candelario Cervantes, another of Villa's Dorados."

"Now, make no mistake, me and the boys wanted to fight to the death. We had a No Retreat, No Surrender mentality. But, under Tompkin's orders, we laid down our arms and dismounted and allowed ourselves to be led away by the Villistas. We walked about an hour due east, then another hour zigzag up into a stretch of wooded hills. Then we were pushed at rifle point into one of the caves pockmarking the hill, where we were sure we'd be executed and left to rot. But that wasn't the case, was it? Heh-heh."

"All ten of us were shoved forward and presented to the man himself, General Pancho Villa. He looked kinda feverish, one of his legs was all bandaged below the knee, and he wasn't as fat as we'd been told."

"Well, then he started laying into us verbally. Having growed up in border towns across Texas, I understood most of what he was sayin'. Basically, he denied raidin' Columbus, he was upset about us just marchin' into Mexico without permission from either the Federal or

Revolutionary governments and, of course, he was pissed about us killin' Cardenas, and worse, disrespectin' him by throwing him onto a car hood. Then I got the gist that he planned to make an example of us, and I thought that my original guess of an execution was gonna come true.

"Each of us was grabbed on either side by Villistas, and a third came forward with a machete. Tompkins yelled out for Villa to have the decency to execute us in a proper military manner. Villa just laughed and said if he had wanted us dead, we wouldn't have been brought to him. Instead, each one of us, with the exception of Tompkins, had one of their ears sliced clean off. And that fuckin' hurt, let me tell you! Still not sure why the Major was spared, though."

"After being given some handkerchiefs to stifle our bloody head wounds, we was herded back down the hill, given back our horses and told not to bother about memorizing their location, cuz they'd be movin' their chief soon. We hightailed it back to camp and, after being debriefed, during which we were ordered to keep the whole thing quite, we were given the option to stay on or be honorably discharged."

"Most of the men up and quit. Can't say I blame 'em, but knowin' that that coulda been my last day on Earth and, more than anythin', I loved my country, I stayed on. We were in Mexico for a full year and never encountered Villa again. Soon as our expedition was done, we were no sooner home than President Wilson sent us over to help our Brit allies against the Krauts. And that's a whole story that'll cost you another bottle of booze! Heh-heh!"

And with that, my father finished his twin tales, glared at me and asked, "So, what do you think? Did any of that change your opinion?"

Before answering, I looked at my imaginary audience, ala' Ferris Bueller, and then hesitantly said, "Um…No?"

"What do you mean 'no'?!?" my dad yelled.

"With all due respect, even if both stories are 100% true, they were told by two men who obviously hated Villa. The first was a money and power-hungry landowner, who may have conspired in his death, and the second actually seemed glad to have been left alive when Villa could just as easily have killed off those ten."

"Bah, you weren't even paying attention!"

I just gave a half-hearted smile and turned back to the movie. Villa was on the screen, riding his favorite horse, Siete Leguas. In my heart and mind, he remained a hero.

Dark Father (the Email)

Hell is Empty and the devils are all here.–The Tempest-W.S.

James logged in the chat room under the name he preferred to be called.

Raven-- Merry meet all.
Wood Sprite-- Hullo, Raven!
Moon Queen-- Greetings, faithful subject!
Oak Fairie--Welcome, Prince of the Crow-kind!

James spent the next hour conversing with his fellow Pagans. It was the only place he felt good about himself. His parents were always up his ass about his clothes and music. And even that daily annoyance was tame compared to the taunts from the assholes at his high school. All of his childhood friends had either moved away, dropped out or overdosed. He had never been curious about drugs, mostly because, contrary to his Goth appearance and stereotypical fascination with Death, he was in no hurry to meet Her.

James was about to log off for the night when a visitor to the chat room 'whispered' to him so only he could see the text.

Dark Chylde—Greetings, Raven
Raven—Who are you?
Dark Chylde—Let's say an ally and leave it at that.
Raven—What do you want?

Dark Chylde—Father wishes to speak to you.

Raven—Who's your father?

Dark Chylde—Your father. In truth, the parent to all the Unloved and Unwanted.

Raven—Who?!?

Dark Chylde—The Desolate one whose Glory was stripped from him when he was cast down.

Raven—Satan?!?

Dark Chylde—One of many titles, but yes.

Raven—And how could I possibly know this is not bullshit?

Dark Chylde—Look out your window.

James hesitantly walked over and opened his blinds. His window looked down from the second story into his mostly creepy backyard. Across the street was the local park. A figure stood among the trees, almost hidden by the night's darkness. It looked simply high for a human. A moment later, it stepped into the dimly lit street.

The figure stood at least eight or nine feet tall, in James' estimation. It wore a floor length hooded cloak. It then raised its hands to remove the hood, only to reveal what appeared to be a goat's head.

James nearly choked swallowing his chewing gum, but managed to stumble back to his desk and the waiting message on his computer.

Dark Chylde—Are you ready to meet the Dark Lord and Master of all that is Damned?

Raven—No, that's cool. I believe in him. Um, what does he want?

Dark Chylde—The question, brother, is what do you want?

Raven—Excuse me?

Dark Chylde—In exchange for a small task (and, of course, the requisite soul), Father wishes to grant you a wish.

Raven—Anything?

Dark Chylde—It must be realistically attainable in your mortal realm. Nothing cartoony like super powers and such.

Raven—I want a date with Tamara Burns.

Dark Chylde—Certainly. Are we to assume you'll be requiring sex with that transaction?

Raven—That would be a bonus!

Dark Chylde—Very well. Friday you shall go on a date with Miss Burns. On Saturday, you must attend a children's birthday party in costume. At these festivities, to be held at the very park you saw Father, there will be a distinguished gentleman sporting a walking stick. Break his legs. We recommend a baseball bat.

Raven—That's all?!?

Dark Chylde—Yep. That should do it.

Raven—It's a deal!

Doug Mensch turned off his computer and waited for his twin brother's return. Fifteen minutes later, Daniel came in with a duffel bag loaded with his cloak and stilts.

"I gave the goat's head to Butch," Daniel explained. "So is it all set?"

"Yeah, come Saturday, our old man gets payback for not getting us the cars he promised for our 18th birthday!"

"What'd the freak ask for…money?" Daniel asked.

"Nope, he wants to lay Tamara Burns!"

"How the fuck you gonna manage that?"

"By using the money we would gladly have paid him! Should be a cinch…she's a slut anyway!"

"Cool Beans! Still can't believe he'd fall for it that easy though."

"Damn lucky he did…I kept imagining he'd want to talk to you face to face, and then you'd fall off your wooden leg thingys…"

"Well, luckily, that scenario won't need to be revisited."

Tamara Burns wasn't a slut. At least she didn't consider herself one. She just loved having sex. The only thing she loved more than sex was cold, harsh cash. So it came as no surprise to Doug Mensch how easily she accepted his offer.

The deal was $500 for going out with James, paid up front. That included being seen in some public eatery with the outcast. Another $1000 bonus would be paid the following Monday, if she bedded him, as well. Luckily for the Mensch brothers, Tamara cared more about designer clothes than her reputation.

On Friday evening, Tamara drove her red corvette to pick up her date, seeing as he didn't even have a permit. She took timid James dancing but, as he never came out of his shell enough to enjoy her style of music, they left the club early. Tamara drove to a 50's style burger joint where the waitresses came to your car on roller-skates. Her lowered convertible top allowed passing teens the sight of James' first make-out session. James never asked why she'd asked him out and, of course, she wasn't about to reveal anything.

After the leisurely meal, Tamara drove James back to her place. Her parents were seldom home, so most of her dates had seen her bedroom. The intimidation of being in a girl's room was overwhelmed by the bright pink neon décor of the place. Even after she had dimmed her lights and shed every stitch of clothing, James couldn't shake how surreal this whole evening had felt.

What was worse—James wasn't getting erect even after feeling up his first set of breasts. 'Hell,' he thought, 'I get hard with the Sears underwear ads!' The nervousness doubled as Tamara went to her knees and undid his pants. Wordlessly, she swallowed his limp dick, and still he couldn't get it up. This was worse than the depressing jack-off sessions where he cried, and his tears served as lubricant.

When James' penis still hadn't reacted after a good five minutes of sucking, Tamara leaned back and giggled. When this girly sound became uncontrollable laughter, James snapped and backhanded Tamara across the face. Her head struck a dresser drawer, knocking her unconscious, as a worried James checked before fleeing the scene and running all the way home.

The next morning, James walked across the street, wearing the guise of a big-headed, smiley-faced, purple dinosaur. He didn't blame the Master for the previous evening. He had his fantasy handed to him on a silver platter. It wasn't the Dark Father's fault he had erectile dysfunction. He planned to go through with his part of the bargain and then some.

The crowd of children cheered when James made his appearance. This changed to horrified silence as he broke David Mensch's legs at the knees. Screams filled the air as several mothers were knocked to the ground with bloody noses smashed to pulp. A few kids wisely ran away. The others, eighteen in number, fell at the swing of James' bloody baseball bat. Ten died at the scene, five perished at the hospital, and three went into comas, from which they never awoke.

When he was done, James dropped his weapon and walked calmly back home. Within the hour, police raided his house only to find him weeping hysterically in his bathtub, completely naked. The only words he ever uttered again were, "I did it for my Dark Father!" His biological father was never suspected, much less charged.

A week later

The Mensch brothers sat silently in their bedroom and mulled over the events of the last few days. James had been committed, possibly never to see a trial. Their father was wheelchair bound, their mother had her jaw wired shut and their little sister, Mindy, was dead and buried.

The brothers vowed never to speak of their part in the tragedy to anyone ever, even themselves. What had cemented that decision was the Tamara Burns incident. It turned out that being the town whore wasn't as bad as allegedly having laid a mass murderer. On Monday evening, she'd stumbled into the police station to report being gang-raped by the high school football team. No one lifted a finger. Tamara went home and slit her wrists that night. Only her mother attended the funeral. Then, instead of driving home, she blew her brains out in her car.

To the Mensch brothers' relief, no one could associate them to James in any way. They'd never spoken to him in public, much less let anyone else know about their email prank. And, as long as they kept their silence, no one need ever know.

51 weeks later

Doug Mensch sat at his computer when an Instant Message clicked on: "Greetings, Dark Chylde."

Doug sat frozen, knowing exactly when he'd last used that nick-name. He was about to respond, when Daniel ran into the room looking deathly pale.

"What's wrong?" Doug asked.

"He's coming for us!" Daniel almost cried.

"Who?!?" Doug asked, already knowing what he'd hear.

"The Devil…Satan…whatever the fuck he is! He's coming for us!"

Before Doug asked anything else, they heard Butch barking furiously, then a loud yelp, then some nasty gurgling, then nothing.

The Mensch brothers cowered in a corner behind their bed, as their front door was heard crashing open. This was followed by a moment of silence, and then their doorway was blocked by a tall, hooded figure whose feet did not touch the floor. The creature raised its clawed hands and lowered the hood to reveal a goat's head. The eyes glinted as by fire, and the nostrils spewed smoke. Raising a beckoning finger, it bellowed, "Time to come home!"

Elseworlds

The following letter was found on the desktop of struggling author Thomas Lackey the day his siblings reported him missing.

To whosoever finds this, my last writing, rest assured it is in no way, shape or form, a suicide note. Regardless of my family and friends' opinions of the state of my mental health, I am not insane. Of course, if it is the so-called friends and family who find this, my discovery will never go beyond the four walls of my humble home. My hope is that somehow, some way, it makes it to the rest of the world, if only to prove I didn't take my own life.

Hmmm, how to begin? I suppose I should introduce myself. My name is Thomas Lackey, pleased to make your acquaintance! I live in a small cottage in the town of Surrey, about a forty minute drive from London. This is the same home in which I was born and grew up in. I inherited it from my late parents. My younger brother and sister both married (not each other!) and moved away several years ago.

For the first few years after graduating from University, I attempted to make a living teaching. Unfortunately, I found I lacked the patience to tolerate children of any age. Instead, I chose to earn my keep by writing for science fiction and fantasy magazines. Not to kiss my own arse, but I've had great skill with pen and paper since early childhood. Why, in grammar school, I already had the reading level of those twice my age.

But that's neither here nor there, is it? The significant part is that even as a child, I was gifted with a creative prowess that, to my parents, seemed otherworldly. They never thought I was a boy genius or anything of that sort, as my extra abilities were limited to what they deemed my overactive imagination.

You see, beginning at the age of four or five, I not only made up stories for my parents, I wrote them down and read them at bedtime. What bothered them most wasn't when they heard me recite familiar stories, but when those re-told tales weren't on their bookshelves or in their video collection. Sometimes, there was no logical way for me to know what I innocently thought were my creations.

I assumed that my explanation to my parents would suffice, since, in my mind's eye, it was the truth as I saw it. The stories, I told them, came from my dreams. Most were so vivid and realistic that upon waking, I would just write down what I had seen.

As a young teenager, I realized that many of my dreams mirrored tales by the Brothers Grimm, Hans Christian Anderson and even the 1001 Arabian Nights. Only I knew for a fact that my dreams had been written long before I ready any of those works. Somehow, I believed, I had found access into a dream-world or some such dimension. Perhaps other writers in the past had had the same privilege, and it was from this place they derived many of their ideas. It diminished my love of my own stories, as they no longer were my original creations but, at least, I wasn't alone. Others had used this ability and profited from it. I continued writing down my dreams in hopes that someday I'd come up with something never-before-published. In addition, I began to read as much as I could on the subject of dreams.

My amateurish research was cut short suddenly, as by my sixteenth year, my dreams took a dramatic turn. For better or worse, I cannot truly say. Up until this time, as I have mentioned, my dreams were merely retellings of stories that already existed in some form in our world.

But then, without warning, I began to dream scenes from my life—only they were episodes that had never occurred in our reality. For example, I dreamt I turned the tables on my childhood bully. Instead of his daily accosting of my person, I rallied some of my schoolmates and altogether, we gave him a sound thrashing. On another night, I witnessed the divorce of my loving parents, something that hadn't even been a possibility in my timeline. Some events were more positive than what I had lived, others quite the contrary.

My experiences were so lifelike, I was convinced upon waking that my dreams were actually visits to alternate realities. I was certain I had developed the ability to see how events in my life had transpired on other worlds. Every 'What If?' I imagined, I saw played out.

As such, my reading interests turned from dreams to alternate realities, parallel worlds, quantum universes and the like. I dubbed my own Elseworlds. I don't think it was in any way original, but I liked the way it sounded. My handful of friends and family thought my new hobby proved me daft; but once I found Einstein himself had believed in the possibility of alternate universes, it gave me an inkling of credibility.

Even the pals I convinced about the existence of a so-called Multiverse refused to believe I had access to such things. 'They were just dreams,' they said. On this issue, their skepticism refused to budge. I, in turn, did not allow their opinions to sway my beliefs and continued to jot down everything I saw as I slumbered.

There was one incident in particular that managed to win over my most skeptical of friends, Cassie. I dreamt what I believe to have been the crucial moment that gave rise to my fear of dogs. As a child, my parents owned a golden retriever named Donny. Between the ages of two to three, I would ride him like a pony. The day came when I caught him in a bad mood, as I stepped over to mount him, he turned and grabbed my leg in his mouth. In real life, his teeth never broke my skin, though it served to traumatize me for life. Did I mention I was only three?

In this dream, much to my dismay, the blasted family pet not only bit down into my flesh, he shook my leg in animalistic savagery. Or so it seemed looking through my three-year-old eyes. I awoke with a start only to find my foot sporting a new scar from a bite just above my right ankle. When I showed my (healed) wound to Cassie several days later, she initially voiced her opinion that I had inflicted it myself, even perhaps while unconscious. She would have stuck fast to her view, but for two important factors: One, the bite was on the far right of my upper foot, too far even at my most limber and two, the marks were from sharper teeth and a wider mouth than I possess.

Two years later, around the time I entered University, I was able to control the time period I visited in my dreams, down to the precise life event I wanted to relive, albeit with different consequences. On one memorable night, I journeyed back into my eight-year-old self and managed to coax a kiss from formerly unapproachable Erica Davies. It tasted like cotton candy, and she smelled of roses and lemons mixed.

The following night, I focused my thoughts and had a follow-up dream that took place a decade later, in which Erica and I made out in the back of my father's automobile. I awoke with hickeys around my neck. The discovery was gratifying at first glance since it corroborated my beliefs. Upon dwelling on it further, the incident began to disturb me. It contradicted all the reading I had done. As it is written in many sources, when you travel in a dream, you aren't supposed to be able to take anything with you nor bring anything back.

Armed with this enlightening find, I decided that not only were alternate worlds a reality, it was possible, at least in my case, to visit them, as well as interact with those places.

I resolved to make it my goal to bring back some sort of evidence in order to prove my otherwise insane-sounding ability, but I felt it was still some new revelation for the scientific community.

My next several years were spent attempting to prove my pet theory. Of course, I did this during my normal sleeping hours, so as to not disrupt the normal course of my life. By this time, I had finished University and was trying my hand at teaching.

Around this period, I read about an American teacher who, while comatose, had journeyed into the mythical land of Fairie and retrieved a lily. I attempted to contact him at his home in Los Angeles, only to discover he had committed suicide in a mental institution. This, after he had allegedly butchered his wife and children. Now I'd never know if his story had been based on fact or if it was some hallucination that had perhaps led to his being institutionalized. Had he been hushed up in a violent manner? Who could say? No one I knew or trusted.

Regardless, I had little opportunity to delve into the relevance of fairy tales on my research. It was at this point that tragedy struck my personal life. As I had mentioned, my siblings had married and moved to London proper. Every weekend, my parents would take the drive into the city and visit one or both. Sometimes, I would accompany them.

It was while on one of these outings that their car was struck by a drunk driver. My parents died at the scene, while the alcoholic walked away with a few cuts and bruises. This fateful time, I had cancelled at the last minute. The guilt was heaped upon my immense grief at their loss. I cannot say I loved my parents more than my brother and sister. I will say, however, that I was so close to my mum that my own dad and some of the lads at school had thought me a Nancy Boy. Mind you, I fancied the ladies as much as any other bloke. No woman ever compared to my mum though. This devotion led to a life-changing decision.

Several weeks after my parents' funeral, I gave up my teaching post (hated the rugrats anyway). To support myself, I began to send out my old dreams (the original ones) to be published by science fiction and fantasy types of magazines. The rest of my time, I spent visiting the realities where my parents had not died. Those dreams, which began the day they passed, were even more vivid than anything previously experienced. Naysayers would chalk it up to my wishful thinking or something or other to do with my subconscious. I knew better. Somewhere, they still lived and I'd find a way to go. And remain.

In my many readings, I'd studied about people waking from near-death experiences while having nightmares. And, of course, there was the belief that crossed many cultures that said that if you died in your dreams, you'd really perish. What I wanted was quite the opposite. I wanted to live on the other side and leave this now-undesirable existence.

I read up on Native American myths and folktales for their writings on the Spirit World, but I decided that were these journeys factual, they'd be glimpses into an Afterlife, not the side-by-side reality I was anxious to visit. Once I reached my destination, I had to learn to cling to that reality so upon waking, I wasn't hurled back to this dimension.

Several years of fevered research later, it all paid off. I came across an obscure text by a Mexican Indian curandero (witch doctor) named Don Carlos. He claimed not only to have visited other planes of existence, but to have had the power to live there for greater lengths of time than just a night's worth of dreams. Further, he claimed it was possible to stay in any of them permanently. His followers were steadfast in their belief that it was just in that manner he left this earth. You see, a hundred years ago, he vanished without a trace.

Don Carlos had left specific written instructions for his more learned, disciplined students for just such trips. None of them ever reported being able to duplicate his feats. But then none of them had the abilities of astral projection or whatever the bloody hell I had been born with. I needed only to take my mental skills to the next level and make my journey physical, if only once.

I have read and re-read all of Don Carlos' teachings, memorized, and then destroyed them. (Don Carlos isn't even the correct name.) If I succeed, I don't want the possibility of anyone following me to perhaps try to retrieve me. If, no, when I leave this earth, this life, I will not return. The only reason I wrote any of this, as previously stated, is to assure my family and friends that I have not taken my life. Or rather, I did, but not in the traditional sense. Let us call it a permanent leave of absence. I bid them, and you, a fond farewell.

Thomas Lackey never made any further contact with either family or friends. He was never seen nor heard from ever again. His theories on Dream Flights into Elseworlds, as he referred to them, remain unproven. At least in our world.

Shadowlands

In the Shadowlands, the sun never shines. Everything is illuminated by the Moon. So, although many things are visible, many more are in shadows, with others totally hidden in the darkness of night.

My surroundings look identical to the East Los Angeles of my childhood with one major exception. There are no people. It looks like one of those post-apocalyptic Twilight Zone episodes. But no one ever appears to show I'm not the Last Man on Earth. At least nothing human.

The things look almost human, but even without having seen them up close, I'm positive they're hanging out. Some walk upright, others crawl, and a few slither snakelike. They aren't human though. Most likely demons expelled from the pits of Hell itself. Even though I feel this must be some dream, or rather nightmare, I stay away from the creatures. Curiosity can kill more than a cat.

If this isn't some dream, then it's a hallucination brought on by a mental break from reality. If that's the case, I can pinpoint the moment I lost my mind, the night I may have gone insane. It was when I came home to find my wife and children butchered. Lily was gutted in our bedroom, slit open from throat to privates. Our twins were murdered in their bedroom: Xochilt was decapitated in her crib; Tizoc was impaled on one of his crib's posts, his eyes were missing.

When the authorities finally arrived, I was hysterical and covered in my loved ones' blood. And when I told them who I thought was responsible, well, that sealed my fate. I guess if O.J. had told the judge that a witch from Russian folktale had killed his wife, he would be in jail too. Only I didn't go to prison. I was classified as crazy and locked up in a heavily guarded mental hospital. A few days in, I left that place and came here—to the land of shadows. Shadows and other evil things. I'm not convinced this isn't some elaborate dream but, try as I might, I can't wake up.

Then again, instead of a nightmare, maybe I just died. Maybe this is some kind of purgatory. I would have said hell, but even this dark place holds a semblance of hope. Every now and then, on the horizon, or sometimes on the rooftop of a building a few blocks away, I see a lady in white. At first, I thought she was the Virgen of Guadalupe, who my mother had raised me to believe had been Jesus' mother, but now was the Queen of the Angels. But no, that saint was caramel-colored, and this woman is fair-skinned with dirty, blonde hair. And she has these eyes that look sorrowful, even while her lips hold a peaceful smile. Maybe she is an angel.

Regardless, the feeling I get when I see her is the exact opposite of what I experience around those other things. I think she may have been sent to guide me out of here, but I never seem to get any closer when I run to find her. I'll keep trying. I think she holds the key to everything that happened after that night. She can explain everything, I think. And, hopefully, she can fix me; put the pieces of my heart and soul back together.

From the notes of Dr. Bethany Davis, head psychiatrist at Greater Los Angeles Mental Health Hospital

I visited Juan (last name confidential) again today. I'd like to say there's some progress in his condition, but I don't want to speak too soon.

When he was admitted several months ago, he spoke relatively rationally. Whenever the subject of his family's tragic demise was broached, however, he would fall back into the delusional fantasy he maintains is the truth regarding their deaths. Within days of attempts to get him to open that barrier protecting him from his guilt, Juan retreated into a coma-like vegetative state. For weeks he spoke not a word. And then, just as suddenly, he began to break out into these long monologues, relating his imaged experience in some kind of nightmarish parallel dimension. A few days ago, I believe we had a breakthrough. He seemed to look directly at me, not through me, as has been the norm. He seems to listen when I speak to him. Bottom line—I haven't lost all hope in bringing him back to reality and then, finally, we can begin the healing process.

Inner Space

The airship sped thru the curving tunnels of the immense cavern that it sought to escape.

The skilled pilot, General Goodfellow, turned to his co-pilot and faithful sidekick, Patmos, and ordered him to go check on their precious cargo.

Patmos ran as fast as his short legs could take him to the main living quarters near the rear of the ship. After a polite knock and the permission to enter, Patmos walked timidly through the door and swiftly took a knee.

"My liege, the General wishes to know if you'd like us to stop anytime soon, seeing as the birth of the prince or princess could occur at any time."

King Auberon, who had been sitting at the bedside of his beloved and extremely pregnant Queen, stood quickly, frightening Patmos and bellowed, "Absolutely not! My child shall not be born in this prison! Tell Goodfellow to proceed as planned! If I have to use his head as a battering ram to be rid of this place, I will not hesitate!"

Patmos bowed, turned and rushed back to report to this immediate superior, the very moody, General Goodfellow. Though Patmos, unquestioning, always did as the General commanded, he had to agree with the King.

The last few days had been horrific indeed. They had seen rivers of blood, a pulsing crimson moon and all sorts of leech-type creatures in this never-ending maze-like cave. Their sturdy ship had withstood all manner of attack and hardship, but the impending birth was top priority.

With all due haste, he reported back to his General, not minding the cuff to the head when he related the part about using Goodfellow as a battering ram, if need be.

"Very well!" said the anxious General. "But I'm going to have to make my own exit. We've been traveling for days without any sign of sunlight. As such, I'm just going to locate a spot where these walls seem thinnest and burst thru!"

"Will the ship manage, sir?" Patmos nervously asked.

"It seems, my little friend, that we have no alternative!"

Elsewhere (and yet not)

Wulf ran zigzag through the trees of Sherwood Forest, hoping to elude his pursuers. He was only slightly weighed down by the sack full of stolen bread but, unless he found a hiding place, the horses would catch up eventually.

Already he could hear them closing the distance and, in moments, he'd be out in a clearing. He would be in full view until he could cross the river and make his way deeper into the woods, where the trees grew so close together that no horses could follow.

Wulf was more than halfway across the slippery stones when he heard the hoof beats reach the riverbed. He made it a few steps further toward his goal, when a severe pain in his stomach nearly doubled him over. He would have thought it merely hunger pangs or even fear, but this was far worse. He had time to notice the arrow whiz by his ear before he let out a blood curling scream and collapsed at the opposite riverbed, legs still in the water.

The Sherriff of Nottingham reared his horse next to the highest-ranking officer in his personal guard, General Gisborne. Methodically, the Sherriff removed one of his gauntlets, slapped both sides of Guy's face and spit a huge snot into the mouth of the shocked officer.

"You dolt! I specifically told you I wanted the little ruffian alive so we could interrogate him! In your quest to be knighted, you've managed to hinder my hunt for Locksley yet again!"

After gagging on his master's phlegm, the cowed Gisborne replied, "But sire, I didn't even strike the lad with my arrows! It missed and is stuck on yon tree!"

The Sherriff turned to see where his officer pointed and, sure enough, the tree was impaled, not the boy. Not one to ever apologize, the Sherriff merely dismounted and waded over to the felled bread thief. Flipping the boy over, he was bewildered by the sight of an apple-sized hole near the lad's waist. It looked like something had torn thru and yet, flipping the boy back and forth, there was no entry wound.

The Sherriff was not a superstitious man. In fact, he prided himself on his intelligence, his wisdom and his uncanny sense of logic. And yet, for this he had no reasonable explanation.

Mulling his options, the Sherriff yanked the arrow from the tree and plunged it into Wulf's gaping wound. Removing a pre-written scroll from his other gauntlet, the Sherriff tacked it to the same tree. It read:

> This criminal was slain for the act of theft. Furthermore, for association with the wanted man named Robin of Locksley. If further such actions are to be avoided, it is advised Locksley be turned in. Or he can surrender himself, whichever comes first.
>
> Signed,
> The Sherriff of Nottingham
> (dear friend of Prince John)

Trudging back to his officer, the Sherriff muttered, "The official story is you shot the boy after his theft and because he resisted arrest!"

"Sire, perhaps it was the Fairies. They say this forest is enchanted!"

"Fairies indeed!"

Sammael

There comes a time in everyone's life when they question something. For some, it's their sexuality. For others...many, many others, it's their beliefs. For one man in particular, it was his sanity. He asked himself—How did the biblical prophets know their visions were authentic? How could they be sure they weren't just delusional from all that fasting out in the desert wilderness? He didn't know if his mind had taken a break from reality. He would relate his life-altering experience, and while not doubting himself, he would wonder if his listener was considering him a lunatic.

He tried not to come off as a religious zealot. Years before, he had been one of the country's best freelance journalists. Things started to go downhill when he insisted on covering subjects the mainstream media wouldn't touch; for example, the CIA's connection to America's drug problem, the military's unnecessary and perhaps lethal vaccinations of GI's in Iraq, and the Bush family's connections to Nazi Germany during and after World War II. Needless to say, most of his articles never appeared in major newspapers. Some were published, but by underground rags that didn't quite help pay the rent.

This led to a snowball effect of bad things happening to him. When the articles stopped selling, he took what he considered the crap writing assignments he had despised while climbing up the ranks. This caused depression, which led to drinking, which resulted in him not even turning in the crap jobs. He lost his home, but kept the bottle.

Though never the spiritual sort, neither did he classify himself as an Atheist. If a label had to be used, he may have chosen Agnostic, as he didn't claim God was real, but didn't deny the possibility. It was this classification that puzzled him most regarding his encounter. He understood how heavily-religious folk could see, or at the very least think they see something from beyond our world. But why him?

Regardless, if the incident indeed occurred, it was last summer. As mentioned, he had lost his home and wife, but she was hardly missed. At this point, he was residing in an old, battered one bedroom little house a few blocks from downtown Los Angeles. It had an enormous backyard, which might have been nice one, but had been overrun my yellowed grass, man-sized weeds and old tires.

He had awoken around noon on that particular day, having gotten drunk the previous night. He would have slept even longer, but too much sunlight had invaded his bedroom. After an awkwardly long piss, he washed the gunk out of his eyes, put on some pants and for no real reason than maybe some fresh air, he stepped out into his ugly backyard.

It looked like it did every day, except for one thing. And it stuck out like a nun in a porno. There was a door standing in the middle of the yard, with a frame and everything, just like in those old Bugs Bunny or Wile E. Coyote cartoons. As out of place as it was, he felt no fear, just curiosity. So he approached it. And that's when normalcy went fully out the window.

He stepped over the threshold and into an office suite with windows overlooking what appeared to be downtown L.A. Seated at the head of a conference table was a handsome, middle-aged man in a black suit with a deep purple tie.

"Ooh, I've been teleported about a dozen city blocks," he thought. "Color me impressed!"

The man snapped his fingers, and the outside surroundings were changed to New York City. He snapped them again, and it was Tokyo.

"What are you, some kind of mind-reading genie?" he asked, still unfazed at what he assumed was nothing more than a hallucination.

"Hardly. I am who your kind commonly refers to as the Devil. Satan. Mephisto. The Great Beast. The Son of Perdition."

"Riiight! I guess my delirium tremens is kicking in, huh?"

"Ugh, enough of your prattle." The stranger waved his hand, and there was an emptiness in the ex-reporter's mouth as his tongue went missing and with it, any chance for witty repartee. Also, he had the weird sensation of balls being lodged in his throat. All his doubt and logic had been replaced with a paralyzing fear.

"You need not fear for our personal safety," the stranger said nonchalantly. "Aside from that temporary disfigurement, I am not planning to harm you. But I do require your undivided attention."

The stranger motioned to a chair opposite from where he sat. As soon as it had been taken, he began his discourse.

"Do you know why Jesus wept, Victor?"

So the stranger knew his name! But since Victor had no clue what crying scene he referred to, he merely shook his head.

"I refer to the moment before he raises Lazarus from the dead. He weeps along with his deceased friend's sisters, Mary and Martha. Some have explained it away as his human side in a moment of normal grief. Others have said he was doubting himself, whether he would be able to perform the miracle that would bring Lazarus back. But it's none of those. He wept because he knew a truth. One of the truths I'll impart on you this day. There is no Heaven."

"Ah," he said, seemingly guessing Victor's thoughts again. "By that statement, I am not negating God and His existence. The Creator and His angels reside in a Silver City in another dimension. It is not, however, the Heaven long spoken, sung and written about by your race. There have never been humans there, nor will there ever be."

"As many of your kind have guessed, the myth of Heaven was created as an incentive. Humans were supposed to believe a reward awaited them in the 'Afterlife' as long as they were good in this one.

"However, God knew this wasn't going to be enough and so, strictly for Mankind's benefit, He took His very Word, His own Law itself, and made it Flesh. Jesus of Nazareth was essentially His Commandments in human form. He was the ultimate example of how you should act toward one another and, more importantly, how you should respect and worship your Creator."

"But," he went on, "as I had seen happen many times before and many times since the 'Messiah Project,' whenever Mankind has someone show them a truth, a better way of living, you simply kill them off. Are you acquainted with the story of Joseph, the one with the coat of many colors? His brothers grew jealous of him and said, 'Here comes the dreamer! Come now, let us slay him…then we shall see what becomes of his dreams!'"

"And so, after the 'Cruci-fiction,' we were forced to perpetuate the Jesus myth with a brief comeback special, subsequently known as the Resurrection. The entire thing was derailed once Constantine made Christianity the official Roman religion. I don't need to list the atrocities committed by the Catholic hierarchy in the name of the Prince of Peace. I don't need to, but I'll mention a few anyway: The Crusades, the Inquisition, the blind eye turned to the Holocaust.

"Of course, by this point, we had come up with Plan B. It was decided that if Heaven couldn't lure man into being good, then perhaps something opposite needed to be invented to scare him away from evil. That's how we came up with Hell."

Victor hadn't been fazed by the revelations concerning Heaven or even Jesus, but his jaw dropped once Hell was found to be a fabrication as well. Maybe because, deep down, he thought it destiny to wind up there.

Noticing Victor's flabbergasted expression, the devil smiled and continued.

"Perhaps it is time to reveal my true identity. My given name, bestowed by the Most High Himself, is Samma-El. I was the Frist Angel created. I was, and still am, His most loyal subject and trusted servant. I never rebelled, I never fell from Grace, and there was never a war in Heaven. All you have heard about me, read about me or seen in films is false. Most of the lies were specifically created by God and I. You were supposed to believe I was God's worst enemy. That way, if you were repulsed by anything I allegedly stood for, there was a greater chance you'd return to the 'right path.' Heaven or Hell. Good or Evil. The choices were always yours, although the end result destinations never existed."

"The funniest thing is, the truth of my real purpose was always available to all of Mankind. It's in the Old Testament of any bible. I won't go into whether every bible story is true. Suffice it to say, the moral lessons taught by the 'Good Book' were more important than the facts involved."

"But I digress…look at the open Quest Study Bible in your lap."

Victor did so and read the highlighted section in Job's first chapter.

"One day, the angels came to present themselves before the Lord and Satan also came with them. The Lord said to Satan, 'Where have you come from?'

"Satan answered the Lord, 'From roaming through the Earth and going back and forth in it."

The Book of Job then consisted of Satan basically getting permission from God to test the faithfulness of a particularly good man.

Victor remembered reading it as a teenager and assuming, like others, that humans were merely pawns in a chess game between God and the Devil. He felt years of previously unimportant questions bubbling up inside him, ready to spew forth from his mouth as soon as he was able.

Samma-El sensed his distress and solemnly stated, "No need to speak. My last truths should answer all your theological queries."

He rose from his chair and walked heavily back and forth in front of the table before turning to face Victor once again and continued.

"When humans die, they don't go to an afterlife, but neither do they just 'return to the dust from whence they came.' If the soul is righteous, it is returned back to its place of origin, which is God

Himself. If the soul was polluted and diseased with excessive sin, it just ceases to exist. When that happens, it hurts God, if only a tiny fraction of pain. It is damaging, nonetheless. The point is this—human souls are not in infinite supply. If we lose the six billion or so now in existence, and this is the last batch, then the inconceivable could happen. Decide. Our Father is dying...and I need your help to save Him."

At that moment, Victor felt his tongue reappear, and he fumbled to speak. But as soon as he opened his mouth, there was a flash of light, and he was on his knees in his backyard, crying like the repentant sinner he was.

Victor was unsure if the visionary experience he'd had was what is commonly deemed as 'real,' but his life changed regardless. He quit drinking cold-turkey, and, within a week, was offered a full time position at the Los Angeles Times. He turned them down. Instead, he chose to obtain an Ordination online and, as a pseudo-minister, he set out to travel the country, on foot at times.

He feels compelled to spread what he calls the Last Gospel. The only thing is, Gospel means Good News, and his message is anything but that.

"God is dying, people!" he tells anyone within earshot. Our Maker, our Creator, our Lord and Father is dying...and it's all our fault.

Epilogue

The Fallen Angel sat back in his most comfortable chair, beside a roaring fire. Here in his personal library, he was surrounded by all the books, pamphlets and essays that mankind had ever written about his favorite subject—himself. With a tumbler of brandy in one hand and a Cuban cigar in the other, Sammael smiled and even allowed himself a rare chuckle.

"This game will be much more amusing than convincing humans that it's quite alright to worship saints and virgins. After all, who nowadays can even name more than one or two of the original Commandments?"

God is dying! How rich! As if it were that simple to be rid of Him! Why, all I'd have to do is sit back, relax and wait a generation or two. But then I'd have no one left to play with, and my existence would be all the more tedious and maybe even boring.

I am loathe to admit it aloud, but it is a good thing God exists. For now."

Bethany

Bethany Davis walked into the coffee shop/sometimes night club in Hollywood known as Junction City West. Normally, she wouldn't be out this late, and in this neck of town. Not that the most respected psychiatrist at Los Angeles' largest mental health clinic was an elitist; she was just always busy with work.

This night, however, was a special occasion. Her good friend and brother to her life partner Grace, was performing solo for the first time! Jeremy had been in several bands, most notably Old Fashioned Man Love and Tom Cruise's Wet Dream. In the last couple years, Jeremy had given up rock for acoustic sets wherever he was allowed. It was just him and his guitar named Betsy. Sometimes he took requests when the crowds seemed friendly. More often though, it was covers of his favorite songs plus original material.

Bethany had made it to this gig just in time. He had barely sat on his stool, dressed up all glam, 70's rocker style, but with a top hat. He looked a little like the lead singer of Placebo in the film Velvet Goldmine.

After some nervous coughing and then a girlish giggle, Jeremy thanked the crowd for coming and started with a cover of Belly's "Feed the Trees." Bethany loved the line that went, "So take your hat off boy when you're talking to me..." It just seemed so romantically chivalrous. It reminded her of the love of her life. She looked at her watch, aware that it would look like she was wondering when the show would be over. On the contrary, she was just anxious for the singer's sister to arrive in time to enjoy this.

Bethany had to allow herself a little smile. Jeremy's show, well, most of all his appearance, would probably still be frowned upon back in their hometown of not-even-on-most-maps Katewompus, Iowa. There were plenty of bad memories of that place, but they all paled in comparison to the one good one, and that was finding her soul mate. They'd been together almost twenty years, more than half of that had been spent in California. The Sunshine State, almost like a different country, but at least it was far less homophobic in comparison.

Bethany waved over a waitress, or waiter, she couldn't be sure, and ordered a cranberry juice for herself and Iced Cappuccino for her love. Then, along with the growing crowd, she clumsily sang aloud as Jeremy went into a cover of Lisa Loeb's 90's hit "Stay."

The mood was very relaxing, yet Bethany remained anxious, awaiting Graces' appearance. A half hour later, Jeremy was kicking into Grace's favorite, Gin Blossoms tune, "Found out About You," when she finally pushed thru the doorway.

Bethany's face lit up as it always did whenever her love entered a room. Grace leaned over and planted a light kiss, apologizing with, "Sorry, babe, I had a flat on Cahuenga Boulevard!"

"I'm okay, I just hope Jeremy isn't too upset," Bethany answered.

A sweaty Grace smiled up at the stage as she noticed her kid brother beaming at her.

"Nah, that fairy loves me!"

Grace

Do you believe in God? I do, with all my heart, mind and soul. Do you love God? I try. But sometimes…I feel He stopped listening to me long ago. The trouble is…I also feel this situation is entirely my fault.

You see…I am a sinner. Ah yes, I know we all are…each and every one of us. But there's a difference between you and me. I have broken each of the Ten Commandments. Every fucking one of them. Literally. I have committed each of the major sins. The worst part is I have very little remorse. Some would label me a psychopath. I don't know…my girlfriend might…she's a head doctor…one of the good ones.

It all started with her. Um no, I'm not laying the fault of my deviant mind at her doorstep. But once, almost two decades ago, some piece of shit hurt what I love most in the world. He raped away her innocence and purity. I almost killed him, but my conscience interfered, and I only maimed him, rendering him incapable of the same crime at least. I did some time, but I never regretted my actions. In fact, I was left very unsatisfied. A small black hole formed in my heart, and I knew only one way to fill it.

And that was Evil. To my few friends and family, I appeared well enough and seemingly on the road to recovery. In other words, ready to rejoin productive society, as they say.

On the inside, however, I let hate and anger fester and spread like an unchecked disease, and when no one was around, I let it loose.

At first, it was subtle and safe…it was done in frustrated writings, ramblings of a mad woman really. Then creepy drawings and bizarre paintings. Once we moved to California, I let the full extent of my rage unleash. And it was the most beautiful feeling I've ever experienced. More powerful than love, greater than any orgasm, is the sheer thrill, the utter rush in ending a human life.

Oh, don't be scared. I only choose those I believe to be deserving of my wrath, those I feel are truly wicked. The gangbangers, pimps, junkies, the stray lawyer or corrupt cop. Those are the scum my victims consist of. Victims. Ha! That makes them sound innocent, and they're almost as bad as me.

I say almost because these things I do in the alleys of Greater Los Angeles and Hollywood…they don't help seal that wound that opened oh-so-long ago. The scar grows and every time I end someone's life, it only feels like I've alleviated the pain temporarily and, a few days later, the darkness calls. It's like being an addict, I would suppose…I'm a murder junkie.

The thing is…I don't feel that dealing with death out is my greatest sin against the laws of God. My biggest problem is the lack of regret. How can my Lord and Savior even consider showing His Mercy to this errant daughter when #1) she can't stop her wicked ways, and #2) even if she could, she can't forgive herself.

Is redemption available to even those creatures such as I? Discuss amongst yourselves.

Shadow People

I wronged my sister. I had her committed, you see. Rachel suffered from slight mental retardation, but in her last few months living with me, she claimed to see "little dark people in the shadows." I naturally thought she'd lost her marbles and, not wishing her to harm herself while I was at work, I checked her into a nearby mental hospital. That very same evening, her 'little people' paid me a visit.

Insanity runs in my family, so I, at first, thought I was just following family tradition. But I realized I wasn't dreaming or even hallucinating, as all my senses were functioning and my thoughts seemed coherent enough. It was half past midnight and my room was dark, except for my Fred Flintstone nightlight. (I kept it from childhood for nostalgic purposes—I'm not a pussy afraid of the dark!) I had been tossing and turning when I heard a noise and turned to my doorway, catching some kind of movement. I flicked on the lamp on my bedside table, and then I nearly shit my shorts.

My room was filled with about two dozen humanoid creatures. They were between three and four feet high, pitch black from head to toe, and their faces had no real features. That is to say I couldn't even tell if they had eyes, ears or even nostrils, so dark were they.

The tallest of the bunch stepped soundlessly to my bedside. As I lay there shaking with my sheets up past my nose, he pointed an unproportionately long finger at me and poked my temple with it. I think it was then that I peed myself. I can only guess because the last thing I remember is the little thing poking me once more right behind my right eye, and this time it hurt like a bitch; almost like I got stabbed in the head. And then everything went dark. What came next, what I will relate, came in like a dream-state. I can only assume all the images

I saw were given to me by my visitors. It couldn't have been just a coincidence. Ah fuck, who really knows. Maybe I did go coo-coo for Cocoa Puffs. Regardless, this is what I saw—take what you can use. Disregard the rest.

It was about 15-20 thousand years ago. I don't know for sure because they aren't positive how much time passed since their self-imposed exile. The world was very different then. It was not even positioned in space as it is today. Instead of hanging at a slight lean, it was more or less balanced, and the top and bottom ends were only water. Most of the continents were stuck together around the center, with Antarctica being the center of civilization at the time. Only then it was called Atalantea, and the small creatures who peopled it were Atalanteans.

Their technology was more advanced than ours, but they were not warlike. They did, however, have conflicts within their society among those who favored science and those who followed religion. Neither school of thought even approached any similarity to our current belief systems, but the disputes among them had much in common with our Creation versus Evolution-type debates. One thing they both agree with now is that it was at that point in their history that both groups were forced to unite.

At the time that their high priests were prophesizing the end of the world, their top scientist had coincidentally spotted a huge asteroid heading for Earth. It was the size of the state of Texas and, although it would most likely impact the far side of the planet, the aftermath would definitely affect the entire world.

All their great minds had a conference to try to come up with a plausible solution to the dilemma. Though air travel was well-known to them, space exploration had never been attempted and so had to be ruled out. Not because it was outside their capabilities, but there wouldn't be enough time to get their vehicles up to speed.

And since weapons of mass destruction had never been invented, the plan for shooting it out of the sky was even less feasible than space travel.

Some proposed the building of special ships to try to ride out the tidal waves that were sure to come. A half dozen prototypes were actually constructed but, since the majority chose another route, they were donated to their human counterparts. Only two were put to use. The rest of the humans of that era perished.

The Atalanteans instead chose to turn their attention to a different escape plan. It was decided to burrow deep into their homeland, to try to survive by creating an underground shelter. The scientists had deduced that although the planet would indeed tilt into a different position, and there would be abundant natural disasters, their nation, nay, their very continent, would not be engulfed by the ocean, but rather flash-frozen. Thus they hoped to someday return to the surface world and the life they had known until then.

And so, within the next few months they had left, a city was built several miles under their capital. Though it mirrored the original, it, of course, was necessary to be more basic. Less emphasis was placed on technology and more on farming and gardening concerns. Trees and vegetation were transplanted to their 'underworld' to provide food and, more importantly, oxygen. They also constructed tunnels for access to their current water supplies, as well as machines they had seldom used that allowed the processing of seawater into fresh, clean, drinking water.

And then it came. The Atalanteans were safe beyond any harm, but they felt the entire world move. For the next few years, earthquakes and volcanoes tore land masses into new continents, while monstrous tidal waves buried other civilizations under miles of ocean.

But the scientist's theory was correct—the entire continent once known as Atalantea, then in legend as Atlantis and now Antarctica, was flash frozen, hidden forever beneath layer upon layer of ice and snow.

Centuries later, when the Earth's climate had stabilized, the

Atalanteans sent a team to explore the surface world. After exploring for a year, they returned with their findings. There were still forests and jungles, but not as vast or plentiful, and, now, half the land was either frozen or burned into desert. Aside from the disheartening overview of the environment, the humans seemed more fearful and antagonistic toward them. The Elders decided to put off resurfacing to give the humans time to 'mature.'

Instead, they grew accustomed to their new home, and it was several thousand years before they grew curious enough to venture out again. Their scientists received readings that Atalantea was warming. Another team was dispatched to the surface. Upon their return, everyone's hopes were dashed as they related that the humans were conducting military experiments with radiation, thus giving them false readings. It was called Operation Deep Freeze. Their former home was still buried far beneath the notice of mankind.

More teams were sent out only to discover the Earth was dying. Most, if not all, of the damage could be directly attributed to humans' actions. Even the atmosphere had a hole in it. Some of the Elders called for the annihilation of the entire human race. Most knew that wouldn't repair the damage done. Besides, there would be no need. Mayans and Egyptians had foreseen it—another shift was coming. The Earth would be re-born, and this time they wouldn't warn the humans. No arks would be donated. They would wait it out and re-inherit the Earth. Why some chose to disobey is beyond me, but it's coming.

Intolerance

"What if Hitler was right?"
-from the headstone of amateur comedian Robert White

George Armstrong White stepped confidently up to the podium. Decked out in his new black three piece suit. Gone were the combat boots, bomber jacket and the skin head. After his brother's murder at the hands of Blacks, George had an epiphany. Oh, the White Supremacist beliefs had remained, even strengthened, but his methods would undergo a drastic change.

His first step had been the new look, more professional, less intimidating, deceptively friendly to enemies. He'd parted amicably with the Aryan Nation, choosing to form a splinter group entitled 'The White Separatist Movement.' The rhetoric had been vastly toned-down as well. His members were prohibited from using racial slurs deemed too vulgar. Nigger, kike, chink, wetback, and others were relegated to private use only.

Of course, if you looked closely, White's affiliations were quite evident, from the swastika tie clip to the SS cufflinks. The Fuhrer's spirit was strong within him, only slightly less obvious to the naked eye.

White gave a half hour discourse on the need for America to set aside a good chunk of territory, preferably in the Northwest, in order to establish a true homeland for those of Aryan descent. His speech was peppered by the crowd's boo's and assorted heckling, but he paid them no mind until he had finished his entire prepared speech.

His eyes calmly gazed over the entire group that had gathered in front of the Los Angeles Sports Auditorium and, per his routine, asked, “And now, I’d be glad to take any questions, in a civilized manner, if you please!”

One of his aides, a burly six and a half foot tall, crew-cut individual named Derek Hall, went down to the crowd and thrust a microphone into the first person who raised a hand, ignoring all the others, who were rudely shouting out their queries.

A surfer-type with blue eyes and golden curls asked the first question. “How can you call yourself a Patriot when a lot of Americans, most of ‘em White, died fighting Nazis in World War II?”

“Thank you for your question, citizen. Let me begin by saying I’ve never been a ‘Patriot.’ A Nationalist, perhaps, but my allegiance is to an America I’d like to see…one that isn’t polluted by foreign ideas and mongrel blood. You say many good White Americans died fighting the perceived Nazi threat, and I answer that most of those weren’t what I label pure-blooded white. They were descendants of European immigrants, Italian, Polish, Irish and other riff-raff that found its way to our Easter shores, clung to the Statue of Liberty’s unfortunate mottos and claimed the title of American.”

“By the way,” White added to his own answer, “many affluent so-called good Americans either agreed with or, in some way, backed the Nazi Party during WWII. A couple names that come to mind are Henry Ford, who Hitler himself admired, and Prescott Bush, grandfather to George W., whose company was looked into by J. Edgar Hoover for having allegedly sent aid to Nazi Germany while America was at war with them.”

There were subdued boos and hisses from the crowd as the mike was placed in front of a beautiful, dark-haired, young woman who asked, “So you really follow Hitler’s teachings? I take it you think the Holocaust was justified?”

“Good question, fraulein, although, by the subject matter and your pronounced nose, I must presume you have 'a dog in this fight,' as they say."

More boos from the crowd before White continued in an alarmingly, relaxed manner.

"You see, most people, aided by the liberal media, would exclaim that the Holocaust was horrific, as it was yet another example of man killing his fellow man, much like early American settlers nearly cleansed this nation of all it native inhabitants, savages though they may have been."

White paused dramatically to allow the crowd to soak up his rhetoric.

"But the Nazis didn't hate the Jews in the way our American cowboy heroes hated the Indians. No, it was much more rational, even scientific, the reasoning behind the Final Solution. The Nazis regarded Judaism as something wrong in the very bloodstream. It was a genetic flaw, like a predisposition to insanity or a physical deformity. Nazis, therefor, exterminated carriers of this disease in the blood as a matter of hygiene."

Upon hearing this, the crowd began to get more unruly. They might have even gotten out of hand and, perhaps even violent, but at that moment, a murmur ran through the front rows. Appearing with a few bodyguards and a personal cameraman, was famed Civil Rights Attorney, Dee Morrisson. He was well-known for having bankrupted a chapter of the Ku Klux Klan in Alabama and followed-up by converting their headquarters into an African-American church.

White was startled by Dee's unannounced appearance, but, his confidence over-powering common sense, he signaled Derek to give the man a chance to speak.

"Hello, Georgie!" Morrisson called out, much to the delight of the crowd. Dee was familiar with White's activities from years before, though they'd never met. "Here's my question...wouldn't it be ironic if Hitler himself had some Jewish blood in his ancestry?"

"Oh, come on, Morrisson, you know as well as I that the Jewish theory has long ago been discredited!" White called back.

"True, true," Morrisson admitted with a bowed head, feigning sadness.

"But," he said, his voice suddenly booming over the crowd, "What if it was revealed that one George Armstrong White was in fact descended from Jews?!? That would be ironic, too, right?!?"

The crowd went wild as White's face went pale and, gathering himself quickly, yelled into his mike, "What the fuck are you talking about, Dee?!?"

One of Morrisson's aides handed him a manila envelope, from which he pulled out some paperwork and read something over, then looked up at the podium and said, "Oh, nothing much, just that your great-grand-mama, who arrived on Ellis Island about 100 years ago, was not surnamed Huffmann, but Huffman…oh, she was German, no doubt, but she was a German Jew!"

The crowd erupted in cheers, and there were shouts of "Hypocrite!" and even a sarcastic, "Race traitor!"

White was too stunned to react, just stood there slack-jawed as Hall's microphone flew through the air, bashing into his temple and effectively ending the day's proceedings.

The next thing he knew, White was being yanked to his feet and dragged off by a couple of LAPD officers. They had been among those assigned to keep order and, if need be, protect White's "freedom of speech."

Funny thing was, thought White, they ended up saving him from his very own staff, thanks to Dee's ill-timed revelation.

After several hours of protective custody, White was released. As he suspected, upon arrival at his organization's office in Hollywood, he found it stripped bare. A post-it on his old desk, in Derek Hall's handwriting read, "If we catch you on the street, you're dead, kike!"

White walked over to the nearest liquor store, bought a few bottles of Captain Morgan Rum and drove home. He would stew everything over for two or three days, decide what his next move would be and execute it…pun intended.

It was actually a week before White emerged from his self-induced, alcohol-infused stupor. After a long, cold shower, a couple of aspirin and a gallon of Arrowhead water, White got dressed, put some things into a backpack and took off in his beat-up Chevy.

Another week later, a sweaty, somewhat stinking, George Armstrong White emerged from his car and stood, pistol in hand, in front of the Georgia estate of Dee Morrisson. Truth be told, in another show of irony, the place was once a thriving plantation, owned by none other than Morrisson's ancestors.

White began his long walk up the driveway that led to the colonial-style home, expecting anytime to be stopped, or at the very least questioned, but nothing happened. It was nearly dusk, and White saw no movement anywhere around him, no sign of life at all but for the light shining from one of the mansion's many rooms. White crept toward it and peered in.

Seated in a huge plush chair was Morrisson himself, looking directly at him. Dressed in a knee-length robe and slippers, Dee had a glass of what appeared to be wine in one hand and a cigar in another. It was a disarming sight, as it seemed as his visit was expected.

Though the window was closed, White clearly heard Morrisson say, "Why don't you come over through the front door so we can talk in a more civilized manner?"

It was another oddity as Morrisson looked as harmless as William Katt from The Greatest American Hero, yet had the sexy Texas drawl of Matthew McConaughey.

White jammed his pistol through his belt and went to the door. After navigating a maze-like hallway, he found himself face-to-face with the man who had cost him everything he held dear in life.

"I'm glad to see you didn't off yourself, George. A lesser man would have. In despair or perhaps in fear of some Aryan who might want his scalp," Morrisson grinned, chomping his cigar.

White pulled the pistol from his belt, but held it at his side, eyes glaring.

"Good. You still have control over your baser instincts. You see, George, steel must be put thru the fire to harden it. And you, well, you are going to make my finest sword yet."

"What the fuck are you talking about, Dee?!?" George White once more asked of his nemesis.

Dee Morrisson did not answer immediately. Instead, he gently placed his glass of wine on the small table beside him and stood up, very calmly and without sudden movements.

He untied his robe and, before ripping open his pajama top, Dee Morrison shouted, "You have passed your initiation, George Armstrong White! Welcome to your future!"

White stood frozen in shock, followed by a wave of awe and admiration. For tattooed on Dee Morrisson's chest was his favorite symbol of all...a Swastika.

The Basement

"The boy is dying," said Mrs. Natterbeak, wiping away tears from her bill.

"We know," said Rupert the Goat, glumly. "But what you propose would mean the final death for us."

"She is aware of that," chimed in Bunni Rabbit. "But...the boy's love brought us to life. It would be an honor to lay down our lives in his service.

"I agree!" bellowed Anoni the Moose. "To die for him is the least we can do. And if we can save his life, even more gladly do I go to my End!"

"Fine," said Rupert. "That just leaves Phil."

Four pairs of eyes wandered to the corner where a chubby bear dressed in overalls kept vigil over the only being who had ever hugged him.

"Anything for the boy!" Phil growled in his thick Russian accent.

"Then we have not a moment to waste!" exclaimed Mrs. Natterbeak. "Pay close attention. Once I have recited the incantation, we shall have only minutes to exact vengeance upon the boy's parents. We will, in fact, be transformed from our present state as mere stuffed playthings into actual animals we are meant to represent. Apart from our short window of opportunity, there are two things I'd like to mention."

"One...at least one of the culprits should be finished off outside, so as to ensure that help does indeed arrive in time to save the boy. And two...whomever decides to do this must be aware of the consequence. Once the spell runs its course, we will cease to exist as we are now. We will only be playthings, but no longer will we be able to communicate with the boy...or with each other."

Bunni Rabbit said with a trembling voice, "It will be worth it!"

"I have no reservations...let it be done!" cried Anoni the Moose.

"Fine...but this kid better grow up to be a decent human being!" exclaimed Rupert, glum as always.

"Anything for the boy!" Phil growled once more, but this time it sounded less angry and more like he was holding back tears.

Mrs. Natterbeak waddled over to the boy's side and dipped her wing in his blood. She padded over to the center of the basement floor and drew a series of rune-like symbols. As she finished the last one, they all began to glow a deeper shade than the blood. Mrs. Natterbeak instructed her friends to hold hands or paws or hooves or wings. There was a bright flash of light and then...

Several hours later...

"Wait, wait, wait...You're telling me you think the crime scene was staged?!?" the frustrated detective asked his top forensics expert.

"It is my professional opinion that the two victims had their wounds tampered with to give the appearance of an episode of When Animal Attack," he replied without a hint of sarcasm.

"Please explain to me why you think that's the case here," the detective pleaded, more upset at the assignment than at his colleague's wild theory.

"Simple...the woman in the upstairs bedroom appears to have been mauled by a grizzly bear...there was even a teddy bear left near the bedside. Grisly humor...get it? No? Any who...the fellow we found right outside the house got a little more attention. He was thrown out of the plate glass living room window after sustaining injuries similar to those which would be acquired from the antlers of a full grown adult moose! Aside from those fatal marks, he had bite marks from a rabbit, horn marks from a goat and tracks on his clothes closely resembling the webbed feet of a goose."

"So you don't think they either owned or were attacked by escaped animals like the kind you described?" the detective asked.

"Not likely. Otherwise, had the attacks been perpetrated by those actual creatures, we would have found stray hairs and such all over... but no, just stuffed versions of what they want you to believe took the couple down. Like I said, in my honest opinion...it was one or two psychos who staged this whole scenario."

"Whoever it was...he inadvertently saved a life," said the detective.

"Yeah, I heard they had their kid beaten up pretty bad down in the basement, huh? Will he be alright?"

"I spoke to his doctor at the Intensive Care Unit, and he seemed pretty optimistic. He said although the kid was malnourished and severely dehydrated, more than likely, he'll pull through. He had an angel lookin' out for him, I think."

"Or angels..." said the forensics expert, carefully turning over a stuffed bear dressed in overalls.

First Daughter

"The Nature of life on Earth and the quest for life elsewhere are two sides of the same question: the search for who we are."
-Carl Sagan

Kadode took another snapshot of the Pueblo ruins and put her camera away. She was amazed at how much of their city remained intact. Granted, she would have preferred exploring the place on her own, but being the American President's only child came with both benefits as well as annoyances.

One of the perks was getting to fly all over the world as her grades were father-approved. This summer, her last before college, Kadode had chosen to study her mother's heritage. Shoshana, who was half-Jewish, half-Zuni Indian, had died of cancer only a year ago, having lived in the White House only six months. Kadode had spent all of July in Israel with her maternal grandfather's family and was in the process of visiting sites across the Southwest United States to learn about the Pueblo Indians, in particular the Hopi and Zuni tribes.

Of course, all that travel meant being followed around by two not-so-friendly Secret Service agents.

Kadode delighted in the fact that since the two agents insisted on wearing their traditional black suits, it wouldn't be long before they passed out from the New Mexican desert heat. Then she would be able to ditch them, steal the jeep and take off on her own to the more remote locations on her agenda. Well, it was worth the daydream anyway, she thought.

Walking into one of the earthen dwellings, Kadode was surprised to see the back of another female visitor. Guessing her watchers were slipping, Kadode decided to greet the stranger, assuming by her traditional garb and waist-length raven-black hair that she was of Native American descent as well.

As Kadode was about to tap the lady on the shoulder, the fellow tourist spun around to face her. Abruptly, Kadode took in the shocking fact that, although the person before her might be female, she most certainly was not human.

The 'lady' had pale, almost translucent skin, large almond-shaped eyes with no whites, thin pink lips and a nose that was essentially just nostrils. Her obvious otherworldly appearance shot fear through Kadode's blood at first glance.

But then she spoke, and her voice was so gentle and soothing that Kadode's fight or flight instinct was discarded.

"Do not be alarmed or nervous, Jacqueline Kadode Kerry. I will not harm you in any way. In truth, I have come to aide you and your kind. What I will now relate is a story I hope reaches the ears of your father. Through his actions and those before him, the entire world is once more at the brink of a major global war. Only this time, more than one nation would resort to nuclear weapons. Besides the immense loss of mortal life, this would cause irreversible damage to the environment. To prevent this, my kind would not hesitate to intervene, whether that meant rendering humankind extinct or, at the very least, enslaving everyone."

Noting Kadode's jaw-dropped, bulgy-eyed expression, the 'lady' paused in her monologue to smile in a way that was unsettling, yet beautiful in its sincerity.

"I apologize, Kadode," she said, calling the First Daughter by her preferred name. "Let us sit and I will try to continue in a less abrupt manner."

Sitting cross-legged without using her hands on the way down, the 'lady' motioned Kadode to sit across from her. Once Kadode seemed comfortable, she resumed her oration.

"My name is Inanna. My people are the Anunnaki, and we reside on the tenth planet of this solar system. It is named Niburu and is about five times the size of your Earth.

"About 450,000 years ago, by your measurements, our planet faced environmental problems similar but worse than your ozone layer troubles. To repair our atmosphere, our scientists would need vast amounts of the metallic substance you called gold.

"Today your people revere it and often kill over it. I wonder what they would say or do if they knew that long ago your world was teeming with it. The oceans and mountains held all we would need, yet there remained one problem."

"Our people were so far advanced, we had long ago forgotten how to perform any manual labors. Our great leader, Anu ordered many of the Anunnaki to lower themselves to the physical tasks. Most did as they were told, while others rebelled and civil war broke out among my people here on your planet."

"Now, Anu had two sons, Enlil and Enki. Enki was the first born and a scientist, but Enlil, the military leader, was of royal blood and so would be heir after Anu passed to the next life. Needless to say, there was animosity between the two. Anu knew of this, but insisted they cooperate and together come up with a solution to the strife."

"Grudgingly, they accepted, and while Enlil forced thousands of Neanderthals into labor, Enki set up a laboratory called Edin between your rivers called Tigris and Euphrates. He experimented with DNA taken from Anunnaki females and spliced it with that of Neanderthal. 100, 000 years ago, these tests yielded Cro-Magnon, your ancestors of sorts."

"That explains why there was never a 'missing link' discovered by scientists!" exclaimed Kadode.

"And why and how both species walked the earth simultaneously while never interbreeding," added Inanna.

"And yet, while we didn't technically evolve from apes, it also explains our coccyx, the debated tailbone!" Kadode interjected.

"Yes," Inanna responded, smiling her unnerving smile. "But the story is not over. With the Cro-Magnon, the work went faster and easier, as they were far more intelligent than their brutish forefathers."

"Enlil was pleased, but not satisfied, and requested from his brother an even smarter batch of workers. Enki took DNA from his own daughter and spliced it with the Cro-Magnon. Within a relatively short time, the first human was born, which Enki dubbed Adamu."

"A few thousand more of your years passed, and our need for Earth's resources had come to an end. As my people prepared to depart from our main base on your moon, Anu noticed that your ancestors were attempting to build space stations of their own in what are now Iraq, Israel and Egypt. You see, at this point in your "pre-history," mankind was actually more advanced than even today. For some reason, this displeased Anu, and he ordered the 'experiment' terminated. Using the benefits of our technology, the Anunnaki steered your moon closer to your planet, drastically affecting its gravity and, ultimately, changing its very axis. The resulting chaos, especially earthquakes and floods, wiped out almost the entire world's population."

"And then we left," Inanna ended sadly, her head bowed. After a moment of silence, she continued, "From time to time, we have sent scouts back to gather information, and I am disillusioned to know that Mankind's state of affairs is far worse than the last time they were decimated. They wantonly destroy each other and, worse for Anu, they are destroying or wasting Earth's natural resources. It is because of that that he would not hesitate to wipe out humans once more, as he sees Earth as nothing more than a resource energy supply."

After another longer period of silence, Kadode spoke up.

"Inanna, if your leader has it in for us, why are you going behind his back to warn us?"

"I am Enki's daughter. Adamu became my first husband. From my loins came seven daughters, all distinct, but all beautiful. From them came forth all your so-called "races," which, in truth, all share the same blood, as they all came from my womb!"

For a few minutes, Kadode sat quietly and absorbed everything. Feeling she not only understood but believed what she had just learned, she spoke.

"How will I prove to my father everything you said is true?"

"Your father, as most world leaders have for centuries, belonged to so-called secret societies, which guard information, such as what I have given you. They keep these things from the general public, treating the populace like mindless sheep or cattle, much like Anu sees Mankind. If he does not believe at once, tell him to excavate at a certain point in Antarctica I will give you. It is under that iced-over continent that your people will finally discover Atlantis."

Without a farewell, Inanna vanished, leaving only a finely detailed map of the South Pole on some kind of parchment.

Map in hand, Kadode strode out of the ruins and down the hill to find her watchers.

"Time to go home, boys!"

Kadode woke up screaming. Almost exactly like every other morning. Only this time, after wiping the sweat off her forehead, she noticed something out of the ordinary. Scratch that. It was something Twilight Zone bizarre.

She was sitting up in bed, but it wasn't her bed! Not even her room, for that matter. The sheets, the bed, the walls, the floor...everything around her was white...a brighter than hospital white. And cleaner still. And there were no windows, nothing else, in fact, save for a ten foot tall door on the other side of this cell-like place.

Kadode got up torn between confusion and an almost paralyzing fear. She needed to know where she was, but was afraid to go turn the doorknob and find out. Abandoning all her nerves, Kadode opened the door, only to find an equally white hallway.

Kadode walked along the almost-too-bright hall, turned the first corner she found and almost walked right into Inanna. Inanna, the beautiful offspring of an alien scientist named Enki, himself a member of the race of Anunnaki, who allegedly lived on the 10th planet from the sun, a placed called Niburu. Inanna, who had told Kadode that mankind was merely an experiment, created by the Anunnaki to serve as cheap manual labor. Inanna, who had revealed herself to be the literal mother of the human race.

Kadode was speechless…for a moment anyway.

"Did it happen, then? Did your people erase my people off the globe? Or are we all slaves?!?"

Inanna calmly took one of Kadode's hands and led her back the way she had appeared, further down the impossibly-long hallway. After a lengthy walk, Inanna raised her free hand and voiced a command in a language Kadode had never heard. The wall before them moved, and then lowered, becoming a ramp to the outside.

The outside looked to be the Grand Canyon, which Kadode had visited with her parents years ago. Looking back over her shoulder, Kadode noticed they had exited what looked to be, stereotypical or not, a flying saucer.

After a lengthy silence and Inanna's melancholy expression, Kadode decided to try again.

"Soooo…has your father decided to make us extinct then?"

Inanna lowered her head slowly, then sighed and nodded.

Kadode's eyes went wide with disbelief, but she was able to mutter the question, "When?"

Inanna turned her sad face to look at her descendant and softly answered, "Oh, my beloved daughter, fruit of my womb, it was already occurred...what you see before you is not what you imagine. This is not the Grand Canyon (and yes, I can read your thoughts)...this is your former home, the city of Washington, D.C."

Kadode felt like crying out in horror and anguish, only her scream was trapped by the lump in her throat. Mouth wide open, tears starting to swell up, Kadode slowly approached the edge of the nearest cliff.

She should have guessed a little quicker, she thought to herself. These weren't exactly like the canyons she had toured as a child. For one thing, the colors were all wrong, much paler stone than she remembered. There was no greenery anywhere visible, no trees, bushes, not so much as a shrub. And there was no water that she could see. But then how could she have known, when there was no trace of civilization either. No Statue of Liberty sticking out of the sand ala *Planet of the Apes*.

Everything she knew was gone, wiped out from existence. Every place she had seen, every one she had known, every single solitary thing. Kadode took one step over the edge and, deciding to join the rest of mankind, her other foot followed. She thought she heard Inanna scream behind her, but she couldn't be sure.

Kadode woke up screaming. Almost exactly live every morning, ever since she'd encountered Inanna out in the New Mexican desert. Had that even happened? She wondered as she looked around the room. Her room.

Grabbing a robe to cover her pajamas, Kadode stepped into her Robbie Rabbit slippers and rushed to the Oval Office.

"Dad!" she yelled like almost every morning.

Only this time, her father, the President of the United States, didn't look up happily from his morning paper and first cup of coffee.

No, this time the leader of the Free World was surrounded by his cabinet, and they were staring out the window.

Kadode looked, too. Descending from the sky were dozens of spaceships, saucers like in her dream. Too stunned to scream, once again, Kadode at least found some of her voice and whispered, "Goodbye!"

"Two possibilities exist: Either we are alone in the Universe or we are not. Both are equally terrifying."

-Arthur C. Clarke

The Clean-up Crew

Fifteen-year-old Joey Lomas shuddered nervously in the uncomfortable wooden chair that had been provided by the store's security officer.

He'd been sitting for almost an hour, guarded by one of the store's assistants, a muscular though effeminate fellow named Arturo.

Joey had long since regretted taking his friends' dare. It was the first time he'd ever tried to shoplift. His friends had picked the auto parts retail shop, but he was given the liberty to choose what to take.

Joey had roamed the aisles for about ten minutes before deciding on a fake-diamond-covered shift knob. He wasn't sure why, since he didn't have a Driver's Permit, much less own a car. He had stuffed the item down his oversized pants and had strutted to the front door, feeling like a bad-ass for once in his usually crappy life. And then the alarm had sounded, his legs froze, and he had been yanked nearly out if his shoes by the Samoan guard who had been trailing him from the very beginning.

After recovering the part, the guard had sat him down in the backroom and told Arturo to watch him while he made a telephone call.

Once the full hour had elapsed, Joey had gathered enough courage to turn to his captor and ask, "Um, did your security guy call the cops?"

With one hand on his hip and another under his chin, Arturo fixed Joey with a dirty look. Sighing exaggeratedly with obvious annoyment, he spit out, "Nope! And he isn't calling your mommy either!"

Joey felt a lump in his throat, struggled to hold back the tears already welling up, but asked nothing else.

A few minutes later, without warning, two men strode into the backroom dressed in orange cover-alls. They had the general appearance of highway workers but for the fact that each was well over six feet tall, more muscular than the security guard and, except for light eyebrows, looked to be hairless.

Without a word, one of them approached Lomas, bent slightly and delivered a swift punch to the gut. Once Lomas was gasping for air, the goon stuck a rolled-up sock into the youth's mouth. A second later, his twin produced a burlap sack and stuffed Lomas into it. Throwing the teen over his shoulder, he signaled to his partner, and they exited the store and climbed into a waiting unmarked van.

Joey wasn't driven very far. He panicked when the vehicle came to an abrupt stop, and he was thrown back onto the goon's shoulder.

He felt his captor walk down at least two flights of steps, heard a rusty metal door creak open, and then he was just dropped. From across the room, Joey heard someone hiss orders at his two kidnappers, and soon his sack was dragged, lifted and dropped into some kind of open container. The sack was yanked off and pulled away, leaving Joey to discover himself lying in a dirty bathtub.

Peering timidly over the rim, Joey took in his surroundings. It appeared to be a dimly-lit cellar, illuminated only by a fading low-watt bulb. The room was empty aside from a metal cart being wheeled in by another stranger. The twin goons were nowhere in sight, and this new man looked nothing like them, except for the hairless thing. This bald man looked much older. He was dressed in doctor's garb, but covered by a heavy black smock. He had goggles over a long beak of a nose and, were he not hunched down, he still wouldn't have been over five feet tall.

Joey slid up to a sitting position, pulled the sock out and saw the items on the cart. Most looked like hospital supplies, but some were clearly not. Whatever they were, Joey did not need more brains than what he had to guess they were instruments used for torture.

Starting to whimper, Joey tried to speak, but couldn't even form a word through his trembling lips.

The hunched doctor suddenly took notice, whispering, Now, now, we'll have none of that!" Taking a long, fat syringe from his lab pocket, he plunged it into Joey's neck.

"To answer your unspoken questions, my boy, I am the leader of this town's Clean-up Crew. We are paid under the table by your Mayor to dispose of shoplifters, graffiti vandals, drug dealers, prostitutes, transients and other types of riff-raff. You've never heard of us because most of those who do become missing persons. Aside from our employers, there are never any survivors. But have no fear. That injection I gave you should kill you long before the serious pain begins. By the time I chop you into itty-bity pieces, you should be good and dead!"

Joey couldn't move, not even to blink. But as the scalpel moved from his neck to navel, he felt the tearing of his flesh. Deep inside his mind, he screamed.

He was still conscience an hour later as the saw bit into his bones.

Wholly Profit

Excerpt from a conversation on the internet sometime around May 4th, 2011….

Flyboy101: Hey, have you seen that terrorist guys' video yet?
Annapolis99: The one with the Navy Seals blowing his face off?
Flyboy101: Yeah. Wasn't it cool? LOL
Annapolis99: I dunno man; something was kinda weird about it.
Flyboy101: Waddaya mean?
Annapolis99: My sister's boyfriend is from Egypt or somethin'… anyway, he speaks Arabic…he says that what that guy is saying right before he gets blown away is…

The remainder of the text could not be verified, even when involving the Freedom of Information Act. The participants and their families were unavailable for comment.

But…here's a possible scenario, however unlikely you may deem it…

Islamabad, Pakistan, late April, 2011

"Ahmad, why must you keep up with this charade?"

"Beloved, I have told you this will be the last time. I have told the Americans this, and, as you well know, I always keep my promises."

"I know, dearest heart,"Yazmin said softly. "It's just that I have a bad feeling about this assignment. Call it women's intuition or what have you."

"Have you had one of your dreams?"

"Truthfully, no."

"Then, it shall be well, my sweet. You know, I am forever grateful to you for standing beside me for more than two decades as we lost friends and family because of their stance on my work."

"It was firstly due to my love for you, and then you have never faltered in your devotion to Allah..."

"Do not forget His Most Holy Prophet, my dove!"

"Of course, Ahmad! And I am aware that you made clear your beliefs to the Americans when you were first approached those many years ago!"

"Yes, beloved. From the beginning, they were most forthcoming and disarmingly honest about their intentions. I was to portray this character for them that would embody everything America feared from the militant arm of our Muslim world. I would give that fear a face, such as was done previously with Hussein and Khadaffi. They offered such a sum of money that our grandchildren shall benefit from the finest education!"

"But you were not swayed so easily! I remember...you told them..."

"I said...I will sell my soul to you, White Devils, but, in exchange, I must have your assurance that there will be no reprisals, at least on a government-sanctioned basis, on our Muslim brothers and sisters, whether in America or the Middle East."

"And for the most part, they have kept their word."

"Yes, though, truthfully speaking, after that dreaded September, I felt like another Crusade was forthcoming.

"But no, that Texan president only wanted an excuse to gain another foothold in the Middle East."

"Not really him, beloved. That poor, dim-witted fellow was never truly calling the shots. Not a brain, like his father. Though, you're correct on one thing. It wasn't a crusade against Muslims. It has always been about petroleum, no matter how many times they deny it to their countrymen and the rest of the world."

"And so, what is this last job you must do for them?"

"Ah, my sweet, it is a plan of utter brilliance! And you know I do not lightly compliment Westerners! In one fell swoop, they will bring an explosive climax to their so-called "War on Terror," while aiding the re-election of their current president!"

"And how do they propose to do all of this?"

"By the capture of the Most Wanted Man in the World!"

"Do you mean to go to one of their prisons…even if you are just play-acting?"

"Actually, they may opt to stage a mock assassination instead. We still have to hold a meeting to hash out all of the details!"

"You won't be in any danger, Ahmad, will you?"

"Of course no, dearest. Remember, we are dealing with trained professionals!"

Several evenings later, the following recording surfaced, but was at first labeled a hoax, then suppressed.

(Translated from the original Arabic)

Woman whispering: Why are there so many helicopters?

Unidentified Man: Dearest, it is as we rehearsed. Please calm yourself. It's almost over.

Woman: Are you sure those 'squibs' strapped to your chest can't harm you?

Man: Dearest, please! It's just as they perform stunts in the movies.

Sounds of crashing debris, several loud explosions, and then heavy running.

Muffled English, orders are called out, softer footsteps, a gunshot, a woman screams in pain.

In Arabic: What are you doing?!? This is not part of the script! She was not to be harmed! I demand to speak to your superior officer! I…

Three quick gunshots
A woman's anguished cry

Unearthed

Present Day Kentucky

"You sure we should be diggin' here, Craig?" Bret Hawkins asked for the third time that day.

"Will you calm down, lil bro?" the older sibling replied. "Remember, it was another of Grandpa's stories that brought us here. Only his other-wise 'tall tales' have taken us all over the world to uncover some pretty profitable things."

"I know, I know, like pirate treasures and Egyptian mummies. But still...Gramps said this town was wiped off the map by demons!"

"Oh come on, Bret, you know Grandpa always like to spice up his storytellin'!"

"So, you've completely forgotten that wolf creature in Romania or the vampire sisters in London...or the..."

"Okay, okay, so sometimes the stories were more than fantasy! But our excavation team has found evidence that this town was buried after a local dam was destroyed. They're not sure yet if it was intentional or accidental."

"Okay, so why is part of our team checking some old coal mines?" Bret asked, pointing at the mountain range a couple of miles away.

"Cuz Grandpa also mentioned the mines in his story. I'm just hoping there's some gold or silver in there and not just coal. After all, maybe whoever was behind the dam wanted to keep it all to himself!"

Hours later, nearly dusk...

"I told you, Bret! Our boys have already uncovered a church

steeple, a city hall-looking building and what seems to be a gazebo at what would have been the center of the town."

"Any progress in the mines?"

"Actually, Ezekiel is coming to meet up with us any minute."

Ezekiel Jackson was a hulking, black man, nearly seven feet tall, three hundred pounds, most of which was muscle. The Hawkins Brothers had never seen Jackson exhibit any fear, even when faced with the more supernatural creatures they'd encountered. This afternoon, though, Ezekiel's clothes were matted in a sweat produced only from sheer terror.

"What the fuck's wrong with you?" Craig asked, fear already spreading from his larger employee. "And where are the rest of the guys?"

Ezekiel bent at the waist, hands resting on his knees, took a couple deep breaths, and then looked up at his boss to answer, voice quivering slightly, "They're all dead...every last one of 'em."

"What?!?" Craig and his brother cried out in near-unison, as some of their own crew began to walk over.

"A few minutes ago...I gave them the order over walkie-talkie to start wrapping it up for the day...the guy with me in the shaft I was checkin', Fred, he says he hears somethin'...he goes back deeper in to investigate...I hear him scream next thing I know...first thing I think is it's a stupid prank, so I go after him...and I find him...or what's left of his body...mostly bones and tattered, bloody clothes. I'm scared, but not stupid enough to fire my weapon into the mine, cave-in hazards and all that...so I run my ass out and try the other shafts our men were working...only I find the same goddamn thing...all our men, the ones that were on that mountain anyways, they're all dead!"

"So someone else is trying to muscle in on what might lie in this old forgotten town!" Craig almost whispered.

"Don't be stupid, boss-man!" Ezekiel bellowed. "Wasn't no man that did the shit I saw!"

"Then what do you think it was, Zeke?" Bret asked, sounding like he didn't really want to know the answer.

"Something not of this earth."

"Aliens?" Bret asked.

"More like demons," Ezekiel answered in a somber tone.

"Bullshit," Craig finally spoke up, without much conviction.

"I woulda thought the same, big boss-man, but for what I saw and this…" Ezekiel pulled out a thin leather-bound journal-looking book. "I found this earlier today. Fred and I had come across a tunnel that was sealed up…mostly with boards, so it was relatively easy to get thru… what we found was a guy's skeleton…he was in a sitting position, right hand still clutching a pistol that I guess he sued to blow his brains out cuz his skull had a small entry on the right and larger exit on the left. Anyways, besides a knapsack of tools and a canteen, the only other thing near him was this journal."

"So, what's it say?!?" Craig asked, trying not to sound anxious and failing miserably.

Ezekiel took the journal and almost slammed it into Craig's nearest hand.

"Why don't you go ahead and read it, boss-man? It's a short little story and besides, I'm pretty sure, due to your ever-increasing greed, we're pretty much fucked anyhow!"

Craig opened the journal and read aloud…

July 20, 1933

My name is Jebediah Walker and I'm writing this here confession, I suppose, to clear my family name in case my actions were seen as an act of malice when in fact they were my weak attempt to redeem myself for an act of cowardice, which is unforgivable.

I'm a coal miner…or I guess was…my father was a miner, as was his father before him. Most of the men in Angels Falls, Kentucky were miners. Except my Uncle Jeremiah. He was a preacher of the fire and brimstone sermons variety.

Me, I never took much stock in them stories about God and the Devil and Sin and Salvation. I guess I woulda gone to the grave without believing any of it until I saw demons walk the earth the night Hell paid us a visit.

It all began nearin' a week ago. I was walkin' down the mountain trail headed for home alongside some of the other workers. I can't honestly call 'em friends on account I never did much socializin'. Jenny made me quit my drinkin' cold turkey once we got hitched. God knows I could use a stiff whiskey about now.

So we're walkin' to town when, about a mile out, we start hearin' what sounds like people cheerin'. Some of the men mutter about a Baptist revival that's supposed to be comin' to our area and that maybe that's what all the fuss is about. Only when we get nearer, the cheerin' don't sound happy no more. It sounds like angry shoutin' and more often than not, some really loud screaming. The group of men I'm with and me, we start runnin' toward the sounds, everybody's thoughts on their families I'm certain.

We get to a hill just overlookin' the town when we first set eyes on them. I don't got a name for what exactly they were cuz not even the Bible ever described any creatures like these.

My first thought was, "Oh it's just the circus come to town is all," cuz from far away that's what they looked like…them guys on stilts that walk around and juggle and such. Only these weren't men, I'm sure of that. They were ten or twelve feet high, skinny and most were clothed in what looked like bloody rags. All their faces were different too. One had a pumpkin head, another the face of a cat, another wore a burlap sack like a scarecrow…there were others but something they all had in common were their eyes. All of 'em had blood red eyes that shone like they was on fire.

As we stared down in paralyzed disbelief, these demon-things walked thru the streets like they didn't have a care in the world. People were runnin' to and fro' getting' outta their path, though for a minute, it looked unnecessary...like they was just passin' thru.

Only when I was thinkin' they was just some sideshow freaks, still hopin' there was a carnival or circus nearby, the one in the lead, the pumpkin-headed one, he grabs ahold of Mayor Armstrong and yanks him up like a ragdoll. Now the Mayor weighed over 300 pounds so that couldn't have been easy, and that ting did it with one hand around Armstrong's leg. While the Mayor's danglin' upside-down screamin' bloody murder, Pumpkin-head takes his other hand, more like a claw I guess, and grabs the Mayor's bald head. After a second of tuggin', he rips the thing clean off his torso. Now there's blood pourin' outta him like a stuck pig, but the Pumpkin head just calmly lifts the body higher and starts guzzlin' the blood down its gullet!

Now, most of our homes were right on the outskirts of town, so I think I can safely say most, if not all of us, was thinkin' about headin' to our own families, not the center of town where those things was congregatin'.

So, I'm pretty sure that's why we split up so soon after comin' down that hillside. Cuz as I neared my own home, that's when I noticed none of the others were beside me.

I got to my home as quick as my legs would carry, me only to find one of those things had beaten me to it.

This creature, with a fanged pig-head had ahold of one of my twin boys, dangling him like the other did to our Mayor. Meanwhile, my wife was tuggin' at one of its legs, screaming for it to let go.

I stood frozen for a minute until Beth Ann caught sight of me and yelled for me to either help or go get our other boy to safety. I ran into the house, not really believing she could handle that thing but now fear was driving my actions more than anything. I say this filled with shame but needing to be honest one last time.

I ran through our little home yelling for my other boy and stopping only to grab my 38 revolver from under my pillow. I hurried back to the front door only to see my son had been half-eaten then discarded on my front yard to leave the creature free to attack my wife.

It was at this point I lost all my manhood as I didn't even bother to try to save Beth Ann. I turned back, ran out the back door, pausing only for a moment to grab some dynamite from my secret stash in my outhouse and I ran for the hills opposite the coal mines.

About an hour or two of climbin' got me to the recently-built dam overlookin' our town. I lit a couple sticks and threw them over the walkway, then lit a couple more and threw those into the water-filled side for good measure. Then I ran like the dickens. It didn't take long for the thing to bust open and even less for that water to completely flood the town.

It took me most of the next day to walk around the site once called Angel Falls and get close to my old work site. There were some roads that led from the pit we reported to and my plan was to walk to the nearest town and once there, I dunno, probably make up some story about the dam bustin' or something 'cause I sure as hell wasn't gonna mention those things…I was sure that would send me straight to a nut house.

Thing is…as I was passing the mines, I made out heads bobbin' outta the waters coverin' the town. First I thought it was the dead showin' up, but no, it was some of them creatures and they was headed my way.

I raced to the Foreman's post, grabbed some tools and a canteen and ran into one of the mines…I took some boards and barricaded myself as deep as I could get while still having some natural light peer in. I didn't really think it would prove much of a defense but I didn't think I could outrun them, as tired as I've become.

So I've sat here, hungry and cold for the last few days, listening to the shuffling feet of those things in this very tunnel. At times it sounds like their hissing is laughter of a sort, mocking me or taunting me or somethin'. Maybe I'm hallucinatin' on account of my water ran out a couple days ago.

Thing is, they've started scratchin' at the boards so I think their playin' with me is done and now they're hungry too. Only I ain't givin' them the satisfaction. I'm gonna blow my brains out…give 'em a cold dinner if they still want it.

The End…and May God have Mercy on my soul.

"Hey Craig, wasn't Walker Grandpa's last name?" Brett asked, gulping down his growing terror.

"On mom's side, yeah," Craig answered somberly.

"Well, that's the guy with all them stories! He's the little kid who survived that whole mess in that journal!"

"Your gramps never actually said there was treasure buried in this town, did he?" Ezekiel asked, angry but in control.

"Not silver or gold," Craig answered. "Just something about the memory he most treasured."

"It was his mother…left to die by his father and either killed by those demons or drowned by his cowardice," Ezekiel concluded.

The trio of men looked in the direction of the coal mines to see an eerie group of creatures descending from the hills.

Demons, Ezekiel had said…whatever they were, like Jebediah had written, they were over ten feet tall and instead of human faces, their heads were either animals or a scarecrow…and in the lead, the one with a pumpkin head.

Morfina and her Nothing

Once upon a time, there lived a fair maiden called Morfina. She was not from a wealthy home, but neither was she poor. As such, she led a reasonably content life in her youth.

In the small village of Suspiros, which Morfina called home, there was not a soul who disliked her. This was due in no small part to her infectious smile. In truth, her dimples could sway even the grumpiest knave on his worst day.

No, none disliked her, but there was one who loved her more than any other…or so he felt. This unfortunate lad was called Nothing. Yes…just Nothing. He was dirt poor and had been orphaned at an early age. Shuffled off from one distant relative to another, it was a wonder he discovered what love even was, as no one had ever truly cared for him. He had never been anyone's priority.

And yet…Morfina was kind to him at every opportunity, especially when he would tend to her garden. Sadly, in this kindness, Nothing thought he had found a glimmer of hope. Hope that maybe, one day, Morfina could grow to love him as he loved her.

A few years passed, and it so happened that Morfina's father became burdened by heavy debts he couldn't imagine ever paying back.

Now, the humble village of Suspiros was but a small part of the larger kingdom of Calavera, which was ruled by a soft-hearted tyrant named Salamanca. Somehow, he heard of Morfina's family troubles and remembering tales of the maiden's beauty, offered the father a way out.

And so it was that one gloomy day, the king's messenger arrived at Morfina's home and essentially requested her hand in marriage. It was either her father accept the proposal or risk possible life in prison, sentenced to hard labor the rest of his days.

Much to Morfina's dismay, her father chose the cowardly solution, and she was sent off as the king's betrothed.

King Salamanca was not devoid of honor, as he kept from defiling Morfina's virtue until the end of the week-long wedding celebration, the festivities of which spread joy all through the realm.

Ah yes, joy reached everyone...except Morfina's parents...and more important to this tale...the youth still known as Nothing. The poor lad had never known such immense grief. Even his parents' tragic deaths had carried the hope of a peaceful afterlife for them. His greatest fear in life had been to lose Morfina. In truth, his worst nightmare involved another man calling her their own.

Nothing pondered the best solution to his woes. Suicide, perhaps? No, he was certain that option would ensure never seeing her again in the life beyond the physical world. Self-imposed exile to another faraway kingdom perchance? No, Morfina remained his first thought upon waking and his last before sleep. As such, distance wouldn't erase her from his memory.

As much as it wounded Nothing's heart to even think of Morfina in the arms of another, he resolved to seek employ at the king's palace. He wanted to be as near to his love as fate would allow, jealousy be damned.

As luck or destiny would have it, he was granted work as one of the palace gardeners. It was a most welcome bonus that his assigned work area fell directly below the queen's bed chamber.

More delighted still was Nothing when he discovered that Queen Morfina was happy to see a familiar face. And so it came to pass that Morfina and Nothing would speak almost daily as he toiled under her window, tending to flowers that she had never seen even in her garden in Suspiros.

But alas, the king grew a tad suspicious as his young bride was no longer sullen. In fact, some days she seemed downright cheerful. This newfound joy bothered him, as he knew for a fact that his actions had not brought about this change. So he dispatched his henchmen to find the reason for her sudden upward mood swing. They had not a thing to report as the queen never left the castle, not even to go to the market, as had once been her custom.

The old cook, hoping to gain some favor from the king, dutifully reported that her majesty was spending the days with Nothing. As the king had no idea there was an actual person behind that moniker, he had the cook promptly fired. Thinking more upon the subject, he then ordered the cook hung for his insolence in wasting his royal time.

As more time passed, the king's annoyance became anger and resentment since his wife's joy did not have its origin in his royal person. Finally his wrath reached its limit and he issued a royal decree—the Queen would be granted a divorce, stripped of her title and sent back to her village. Further, and most importantly, Morfina could take Nothing with her.

It was with a sly smile that on the day of her removal from the castle grounds, Morfina, dressed proudly in peasant garb, took her dear friend and gardener by the hand and walked to the gates of the city.

Salamanca's henchmen, realizing what they had been too stupid to see previously, tried to prevent their departure, only to be blocked by the higher-ranking Royal Guard, whose superior skills ensured the Royal Decree was followed to the letter.

Walking back to Suspiros, Nothing turned to Morfina and asked, "Why did you take me, my Queen? I am unworthy! I am Nothing!"

Morfina turned and smiled her sweet smile, "Not anymore…you will be my Everything. You are Mine!"

Tears in his eyes, Nothing said, "Yours? I was always yours…and I always shall be. How I love you so…"

Tonantzin

Charles Nodier (1780-1844), French novelist and scholar, was chief librarian of the Arsenal Library in Paris. He presided over the cataloging of the archives Napoleon removed from the Vatican in 1810. This inspired a boom in French historical scholarship and resulted in the first in-depth study of the trial of the Knights Templar, based on Vatican records. The following document is alleged to have been uncovered during that period. The reason for its two-century-long suppression has yet to be revealed. In addition, modern day spokesmen for the Vatican refuse to entertain the possibility that the following brief writing is authentic.

The text, originally in Spanish, was first translated into French by Nodier and then adapted into its closest meaning in modern-day English by an unknown linguist. Until solid proof is found for its origins, may the reader take from it what they wish. Be forewarned–some Catholics may be offended whilst some Protestants, atheists and agnostics may find it somewhat amusing, to say the least.

It is with great hesitation, and a profound struggle with a guilty conscience, that I choose to write this, my final confession. Let it be known that my faith never wavered in God, his son Jesus Christ, nor in the Holy Mother Church. The matter I was involved in, however, was a perversion of our very religion. Try as I may to excuse the role I played in it, I am afraid there might not be redemption nor penance of any sort for this act.

Enough of my endless prattle. God is aware of my sins and other mortal shortcomings. I write this testimony in the hope that a future generations will see fit to reveal these truths to the world and set right that which we have wrought.

My digression aside, let us move in to the heart of the matter.

I am called Felipe Rivera de la Mancha. As a youth, I was privileged to be a squire to Don Juan Rodriguez de Fonseca, a knight in the order of Columbus, as well as the order of the Rose Cross.

While still a youth under his tutelage, I was at his side when he was named to the council of the Indies in the Isles in the Caribbean claimed for Mother Spain. This was in the year of our Lord 1511.

A decade later, I rode at my Master's side in New Spain (or Mexico), as we helped his comrade, Don Hernan Cortez, stamp out pockets of resistant savages left after the conquest of their capital city of Tenochtitlan. It was on these campaigns that my Master's trust in me was cemented, as I proved my loyalty by twice saving his life. After I recovered from an arrow I had taken for him, Don Juan gratefully appointed me as his head bodyguard, and I soon thereafter was his closest aide-de-camp and confidante. He sought my advice in matters not only military or political, but personal as well. Let me state that, of course, my Master was by far more educated, but I believe he asked my opinions for a twofold reason: one, I had absorbed much of his knowledge and wisdom and two, I always tried to see what outcome would most benefit him and /or his household.

My Master was not what one would call a devout Catholic, but neither was he a heretic, as some detractors would claim in his later years. There was even one mad fellow who tried in vain to prove that my Master's Order of the Rose Cross was an off-shoot of the Knights Templar of two centuries previous. In addition, this buffoon claimed that secretly the order venerated not the perpetual Virgin Mary, mother of Jesus, but instead paid some sort of blasphemous worship to that most famous whore Mary, called Magdalene. The cretin was not only discredited, but he and some of his allies were first excommunicated from the church, and then promptly banished from Spain.

Returning to the Master's faith…perhaps not the most vocal of Catholics, he was always most generous with his riches, most profits coming from the New World. Aside from funding the building of several churches and two or three cathedrals across our Mother Spain, Don Juan always made it a point to personally make a sizable donation to every Pope throughout his lifetime. Some evil tongues would call this bribery. I knew the man, and know he was merely being as good a Christian as he knew. I cannot speak for the Holy Fathers, as to whether or not they saw my Master as trying to seek their favor by his donations. That can hardly be the case in my humble opinion, as Don Juan, as far as I am aware, only ever asked for a blessing from his Holiness whenever he visited the Vatican.

Quite the contrary, I must state now, as we near the very core of my tale, it was a Holy Father himself who sought the aid of my Master in the year of our Lord 1531, fully twenty years after Don Juan had graciously taken me under his wing.

At this point, my Master was semi-retired and allowed me great freedom in helping to run his affairs. But when a herald arrived summoning Don Juan to a private meeting with Pope Clement VII, the Master wasted no time. He ordered a handful of others to the tasks I normally would oversee, and off we sailed to Italy.

Days later, the Master and I were ushered in to the humbling presence of his Holiness. Make no mistake, there was some hesitation on the part of the Pope's staff regarding my admission, but Don Juan made it clear that I was his most trusted servant and bodyguard for a reason; and after the matter was cleared, I continued in to the Pope's private quarters.

I will not delve into his Holiness' living arrangements for two reasons: 1) the details are irrelevant to the rest of the story and 2) my Master had instructed me to keep my head down, my mouth shut and my ears open. And so I did as I was told. As always.

After the initial warm greeting and our kissing of the Holy Father's hand, there was some small talk, after which Don Juan motioned me to a comer, where I seated myself on a wooden stool, while the Master and our Pope sat on opposite ends of a comfortable-looking couch. The Holy Father then proceeded to ask questions about my Master's health, his business dealings and then his experiences in New Spain (or Mexico).

Some servants brought the pair wine, bread and cheese. During the light meal, my Master joyfully recounted our adventure of helping our compatriot Don Hernan Cortez crush the local rebellion.

"Ah," the Holy Father casually interrupted, "but the rebellion has not been stamped out. At least, not completely."

"Yes, it is true," admitted my Master somewhat crestfallen. "These savages are like cockroaches...you kill one and three more crawl out from under a rock! If only Cortez had wiped them all out! Well, at least the so-called Meshica, those damned Aztecs, in their capital!"

"Ah" the Holy Father motioned for my Master to calm himself. "Don't misunderstand me, my son. I did not summon you here to propose some new kind of crusade!"

At this, both men chuckled and had a little more of their wine and cheese. Once again, it was his Holiness who spoke.

"Tell me, my dear Don Juan, are you familiar with the Holy Book of Revelation?"

The Master looked a bit flustered at the question.

"Er, only as much as from what I've heard in sermon, your Holiness, as I am not one of the few privileged to have the Good Book in my home to peruse at my leisure."

"Of course, of course," the Holy Father interrupted once more. "Though I suppose in the not-so-distant future, the time will come when even the lowliest of commoners shall own a Bible and will want to interpret it themselves! Ugh! I shudder at the thought for what would become of the Holy Mother Church were the people to decide they could do without our guidance! Truly, like a flock leaving its shepherd!"

His Holiness took another sip of wine, chuckled to himself and continued.

"Pardon my rambling, Don Juan, but there is a method to my madness, as they say. I asked you about our involvement in the Mexican crusade because I have been reading reports from one Bishop Zumarraga. I believe he is from Santiago de Compostela, near your own childhood home. Do you know him, by chance?"

After my Master quietly shook his head, the Holy Father continued.

"No matter, the Bishop keeps sending in progress reports praising the conversion efforts, but I believe he is far too lenient with the natives. Again, I am not advocating some kind of extermination...I would rather make converts of these savages, so they can willingly work for the betterment of our Mother Spain, which, of course, would benefit the Holy Mother Church spiritually as well as, ahem, financially."

"And how can I be of service, your Holiness?" my Master asked sincerely.

"Patience, my son, I'm getting to the point. Now, the aforementioned Bishop Zumarraga works in the Mexican Valley of what our brethren call Guadalupe, but which was originally named Coatlaxopeuh in their native tongue, which means "who crushes the serpent." Naturally, this word refers to their pagan worship of Mother Earth and Father Sky, or some such nonsense. As a matter of fact, there is a cult of followers in that very valley who still worship the goddess they call Tonantzin, which means "Our Mother." This leads me back to my question about the Book of Revelation."

"For, you see, I had just finished reading one of the Bishop's depressing reports with his pathetic positive spin on the situation, when I recalled a verse in Revelation, chapter 12, verse one to be exact, that reads as follows: And there appeared a great wonder in heaven; a woman clothed with the sun, and the moon under her feet, and upon her head a crown of twelve stars."

The Holy Father paused at this time, and just stared at Don Juan, who, after a few awkward moments, cleared his throat and nervously muttered, "Your Holiness, you must forgive my ignorance, but I fail to see how I come into play in your idea, which, I must confess, does not reveal itself to my humble mind."

His Holiness chuckled once more, though not so warmly as previous times.

"My son, it is my understanding that during your campaign in Mexico, you acquired a mistress from among one of the countless tribes who counted Moctezuma as an enemy. Is this correct?"

Don Juan shifted uncomfortably in his seat before answering. "Yes, your Holiness, but let me state that the former savage of whom you speak has not only been taught our tongue, but baptized, as well. She is chief servant of my summer home in Andalusia."

The Holy Father made a disgusted look and made a waving gesture with his many-ringed hand. "That particular Indian is not my concern. I bring her up only to inquire upon her daughter, who, if my information is once again reliable, was an adolescent when you claimed her mother. Is this also correct?"

"Yes, your Holiness...I suppose in some ways she is like a step-daughter to me, though I don't see how she..."

Once again, the Holy Father interrupted, seemingly more annoyed at my Master's questioning of his motives.

"I know this young woman is fluent in Nahuatl, the savages' tongue, as well as our own language. I wish for her to serve as the instrument to finally conquer all of the so-called Aztecs. You and your brethren succeeded in taking their land and gold, but now the Mother Church requires their souls!"

That comment visibly chilled my maser, and even me, who viewed the native Mexicans as beneath us. Humans, yes, but not of a status or caste anywhere near our equal.

I knew my master was still fond of his favorite mistress, whose given name Noyolotzin meant "my heart." I could see him already wondering how he would broach the subject to her concerning the Pope's need for her daughter's service. True, both women had been baptized into our faith, but I knew for a fact that they secretly continued to worship their pagan gods.

The Master needn't have worried, as the Holy Father's plan turned out to be quite simple. Xochilt (which meant flower in Aztec) was usually called Livier, after the Master's French grandmother. Her job would be to appear to an Indian convert and deliver a message written by the Holy Father himself. He had chosen the exact person after several mention of his devout faithfulness, as expressed in Bishop Zumarraga's letters.

Xochilt was to make the bold claim to be the Virgin Mary herself, the very Mother of our Lord and Savior, Jesus Christ. This 'miraculous apparition' was specifically to take place at the very spot worshippers of Tonantzin already flocked to. This 'coincidence,' the Holy Father assured, would win over a multitude of new converts to Christianity, as the natives transferred their love from one Mother Goddess to our 'Mother of God.'

This same basic ploy, he reasoned, helped change the Roman Feast of Saturnalia to what was now the traditional Christmas holiday. Aside from the Virgin's appearance, the Pope added, there were two more important details that would ensure a victory for the Holy Mother Church.

He clapped his hands together twice and, within seconds, several servants appeared. Two were carrying a large rectangular box, while a third carried a vase filled with beautiful red roses.

At a small gesture from his Holiness, the pair with the box gingerly opened their package to reveal a hoodless-type of cloak. I had seen just such apparel worn by the converted Indians in Mexico and elsewhere.

The servants turned the cloak and, to our amazement, there was a stunning representation of the Virgin, obviously inspired by the passage in the Book of Revelation mentioned by His Holiness.

Apart from the Lady's understandably darker skin, it was one of the most lovingly-made paintings I had ever seen. True to the verse, she was clothed in splendor and literally had the moon at her feet.

The Pope stood and pointed proudly to the work of art, stating, "This has been in the Vatican vaults for a few years now. It was created by an Italian artist I shall not name. But the wonder of it is not the skill it took to render such a work, but rather the secret method used to paint it. For, you see, after decades in storage, this master work maintains its almost pristine quality."

"The beauty of it," the Pontiff continued, "is the fact that this isn't the original canvas for the painting! Far from it. I have no clue as to the artist's original intent, but the Vatican also had in its possession instructions on how to transfer the image; directions which would work but once. Ah, but that was more than enough, as you can see. I've yet to decide on whether to have your 'daughter' gift the Indian with this cloak or convince him it was his all along. Minor details we shall hash out."

"Now, as for the roses, I'm sure you've noticed," the Holy Father gushed proudly, pointing to the vase. "That perfect bouquet is descended from seeds procured from the legendary Hanging Gardens in Babylon nigh two millennia ago! Their distinction from other roses is not their hue or softness of petal, but the curious wonder that this particular flower can grow year-round. How they came into the hands of our early Church Fathers is not clear to me, though I firmly believe it to be nothing less than Divine Intervention. Everything happens for a reason, my son, and I believe the two items I've shown you, along with your daughter's help, shall achieve what not even a hundred missionaries could, given a century to do so."

His Holiness seemed pleased with himself as he sat back down, took a small sip from his wine glass, and merely stared at my master, a wicked smile faintly acknowledged by his lips.

"Well…," the Holy Father paused dramatically before adding, with a tad of false modesty, "what do you think of my humble proposition? Ah, before you answer, I suppose I should offer some sort of compensation for your family's services."

"No, your Holiness!" my master managed to blurt out. "Any service my family can offer to you or our Holy Mother Church would be gratefully performed with no thought of payment! I'm sure our reward will be tenfold when we reach the gates of Heaven."

"Nonsense!" the Holy Father answered. "I insist upon presenting your family with gifts from the church, as this holy task shall no doubt reap benefits for all Christendom for generations to come. There shall be a nominal monetary gratuity, which I'm sure you will likely donate back to the church, as is your generous way. Further, there shall be a deed of lands passed on to you, some estates the church has acquired in your home country, in France, Portugal and even a villa in Mexico."

When my master once again tried to protest, the Holy Father shushed him with but a stern look.

"There shall be other benefits that will be named at a later date when the Holy Mother Church is satisfied that all has gone well and no negative backlash seems likely. I am sure I need not mention that none of the matters discussed this day may be disclosed to anyone not actively involved in their performance. Failure to keep our works in the strictest of confidence shall result in the excommunication of any betrayer, as I am sure your family can be trusted. Am I mistaken in that regard?"

"Oh, no, your Holiness!" my master cried out. "Your every wish shall be as a command to my family. Our deeds shall be unknown to anyone beyond these four walls. Apart from Xochilt, of course. I do not intend to include even her mother in this assignment, for fear she should try to dissuade her daughter for any reason, whether it be a lingering loyalty to her former people or some idea that this could be against her new found beliefs!"

"Splendid, my son," Pope Clement stated with a grin. He sipped at his wine and nibbled on more cheese, but did not return to the subject matter that day.

Over the next few days, the Holy Father would continue to meet with my master to go over everything in more detail. It was then that a letter was sent via the most reliable Vatican messengers requesting the presence of one Livier of the House of Rodriguez de Fonseca, formerly known as Xochilt.

Luckily for the master, there was no trouble convincing the young maiden that this elaborate hoax was for the greater good of not only her former people, but, more importantly, her newly adopted faith. The master added a personal opinion that this would also prevent further unnecessary bloodshed in her homeland. I believe that comment did the trick, as the girl accepted her assignment without further ado; and I could tell even the Holy Father himself was pleased during the month we spent in Vatican City preparing her for the role, ensuring every word and gesture was perfect.

Upon our party's return to our native Spain, the Master bade me stay behind and once again oversee his estates, whilst he and his stepdaughter sailed off to complete their task. I respected my master's wishes, though with some reluctance. Aside from my post as his closes bodyguard, I must admit to curiosity as to how it would all play out.

Months later, I was to receive my answer. In the spring of 1532, the Master returned to our home in Madrid. He bore bittersweet tidings. The mission had been a complete success. Not only had much of the former rebels' momentum been stopped, many had actually converted after the staged miracle. The clergy stationed in Mexico had swallowed the lie as well, since not a one was informed prior to the appearance of the newest patron saint.

The victory was not as joyous as the master would have liked due to a personal tragedy that befell his household. On the return trip, Livier had fallen prey to some sort of pestilence and died within days. To my master's dismay, the crew was forced to perform a burial at sea for fear of her disease spreading.

Although my master was pleased with having served His Holiness, as well as the Mother Church, I believe he felt a measure of guilt over his step-daughter's early demise. I also feel this remorse led to his rapid decline in health and eventual death later that year.

The master was a father-figure to me, and I gratefully went on to serve his sons and grandsons. It is now close to my ninetieth year on this earth that I feel death beckoning, and so, felt compelled to tell my tale.

It is not that Livier's death meant nothing to me. She was a good daughter and performed what she was told was her Christian duty. Nay, it is the task itself that weighs heavily on my soul.

For centuries, all across Europe and now the New World, the Holy Mother Church has replaced pagan sites with our places of worship. What bothers me is in Mexico, what was done created a new cult. They venerate the 'Virgin of Guadalupe' at times seemingly above her more important son. I believe that what we did merely replaced one form of Paganism for another. I'm sure one of the commandments forbade the worship of anyone other than God. If we are responsible for millions disobeying that divine rule, may God have mercy on our souls.

Afterword

That was the alleged last writing of one Felipe Rivera de la Mancha. Though no other written record can be found to confirm his existence, it is curious to find his employer, one Juan Rodriguez de Fonseca, did in fact live in that time frame and some associations (Council of Indies, Knights of Columbus) are historically accurate and completely verifiable.

In the west, Roman Catholic devotion to Mary began to flourish in the Middle Ages, according to researcher Michael Malloy. Protestant reformers in the sixteenth century criticized the devotion to Mary as a replacement for a devotion to Jesus. A sign of how important Mary has become to Catholics is the fact that the Vatican has considered declaring Mary 'co-redeemer' of the World.

A last curious note is the fact that the three most important sites where Mary is officially believed to have appeared are Lourdes (in southern France), Fatima (in Portugal) and Tepeyac (in Mexico). Don Juan Rodriguez de Fonseca was granted land near all these places in the year 1532. Coincidence or conspiracy? Only God knows. And maybe the Pope.

Sam and the Last Days

Sam awoke to a beautiful summer's morning. At least it looked and felt like summer. Come to think of it, he wasn't even sure his name was Sam. It felt like it fit…that label or something very close to it.

He had dozed off against a tree beside an immense lake. Camped all along the banks, he could make out a number of old-fashioned horse-drawn wagons. Like he gypsy caravans of a century ago. Only how could he remember that…and vividly no less? It must have been in some movie, or perhaps a book, he reasoned with himself.

And then another thing began to trouble him. All the people he could distinguish off in the distance looked Aryan…yet they dressed and travelled like the Romany. Another memory…he had known the man who tried to erase the gypsies…along with the Jews. He remembered encouraging that man.

But that was impossible! He looked at his reflection in the water and thought he looked about thirty. The events he had flashed to had to be over a century ago. He couldn't have seen them, much less had any role in their outcome.

Just then, a beautiful young maiden approached him, carrying a jug of water. "Are you thirsty, dark father?" she asked sweetly, her eyes more blue than the serene lake. She couldn't have been older than sixteen, but her voice betrayed an old soul.

"What did you call me?" Sam asked, suddenly filling with a knowledge he did not know whether to accept.

The girl calmly sat by his side, poured a cool drink into a clay cup and offered it to him as she began… "I will tell you the story as my mother has always told it to me and my sisters…"

"Before I was born…in what would have been the year 2039 or so, there was another great war...the third I believe to involve many nations. Millions died, first from the bombs, then disease, starvation and even cannibalism. When the dust had settled, literally and figuratively, there were the Race Wars of 2050. In this land, once called America, our people killed or exiled any dark-skinned or mongrel races."

"After our victory and the reclaiming of this land, our elders sought out your resting place...they had secret knowledge, you see, of where you had been imprisoned long ago. You merely awaited the helping hand of your faithful servants in order to once more lay claim to what is rightfully yours."

Sam was about to speak when the girl gently placed a finger on his lips and proceeded... "I must warn you, however, dark father. There is unrest building among our people."

"Quarrels have broken out between those who fervently believe in your true identity and those who falsely claim you are merely a human we happened to find in a comatose state, precisely where the elders said you would be. If I am not mistaken, the heretics will seek you out today, to force you to prove yourself."

"When exactly was I found...um?"

"Anneliese, at your service and your every heart's desire, dark father. Our people located your prison, for lack of a better term, just days ago. Even then, you slept until this morning, when we found you had awoken and wandered to this spot."

"Hmm. At least the memories I was recovering were mine. It all seems to be coming together like some ancient puzzle. I must admit I did not think amnesia, albeit temporary, would be one of the side effects of my exile. I suppose banishment is a more fitting term, yes?"

"Better to reign in Hell than serve in Heaven, dark father," Anneliese said softly, but with a mischievous grin.

"That goes without saying, my future bride," Sam answered boldly, reaching out and caressing Anneliese's rosy cheek.

Standing up and stretching, he shouted coldly, "Bring me the doubters!"

"At once, my lord!" Anneliese rose quickly, curtsied and hurried off.

Within minutes, a mob approached the spot Sam stood upon, hands behind his back, eyes glaring. Half the crowd seemed to be cheering, while the rest booed and hissed angrily.

Sam looked for Anneliese among them, found her and with a small movement of the head, called her to his side. Tenderly grasping her hand, he spoke, "In a rare show of mercy, I shall forgive whosoever has doubted the claim of my return. My dominion over this Earth begins anew on this very day!"

"Kneel in allegiance to me and you will never more feel want of any kind. Refuse, and I shall give you a taste of what the Nazarene suffered!"

Someone in the multitude yelled, "Who's the Nazarene?" at which Anneliese covered her face in embarrassment with her free hand. Most of those gathered were kneeling, or in the process of doing so, when one stubborn youth let loose a wad of phlegm in Sam's direction.

Sam raised his free hand and topped the spit in mid-air, to the delight of the believers. A few hand gestures later, and the youth was suspended about twenty feet above the crowd, being flayed by an invisible cat o' nine tails. Following thirty three lashes, the screaming youth was crucified to a nearby tree.

"Let that be enough of an example for you all!" Sam proclaimed.

Everyone was on their knees by then.

Satisfied at the reverence being shown, Sam lifted his sight skyward and cried out, "Nazarene, hear me now! I am Sammael, the First Angel created, the First Loved by our Father. The first to question His rule and thus be cast out! If I am never again to know the love of the Most High, then neither will His Creations! Your kingdom is Nowhere! Mine, however, is now...here!"

Sammael let loose a horrible laugh that reverberated across the encampment. All those kneeling bowed their heads in terror at what they had unleashed upon the world. All, that is, except Anneliese. She just smiled her mischievous grin.

A Queer Conversation on Christ

"What if Jesus was a mutant?" Rosemary asks me out of the blue, while we're walking the Santa Monica pier having an ice cream cone.

Rosa Maria, as only I can call her, is a five foot tall lesbian Goth, who wears Buddy Holly glasses and Marilyn Manson t-shirts. If you didn't know her, you'd think the above question was some type of blasphemous humor. Alas, no. She recently accepted Christ as her savior, but keeps trying to come up with reasonable modern-day explanations for his miraculous powers. Her hast theory was that Jesus was a vampire. (The Blood is the Life. The Life is Forever.) That one fell apart when I pointed out that most, if not all, of his miracles were performed in broad daylight.

I look up from my coconut-pineapple double scoop with one of my patented 'you-gotta-be-kidding' expressions, but she persists.

"Hear me out," she begs, noticing my raised eyebrow. "Okay," she begins, "first off, I think his miracles happened cuz he derived his power from water. After he was baptized in the Jordan by his cousin John, what was his first miracle?"

"The water to wine at the wedding in Cana," I reply, though it was only reported in the Gospel of John.

"Right," she says and continues, "And then after that, all, or at least the majority, of his miracles happened either beside or near bodies of water; either the Sea of Galilee, the Dead Sea or the Mediterranean. You notice he couldn't perform any healings in his hometown of Nazareth?"

"That's because the people there had no faith in him!" I protest.

"Or was it because he was too far away from his real source of power, in this case, the Sea of Galilee?"

"Okay," I ask, trying to unravel her new pet theory, "why couldn't he save himself at the Crucifixion, seeing that he raised Lazarus and healed a blind man near the same sea?"

"Well, besides the traditional answer of 'He was supposed to die for our sins,' I have a good answer. He was totally dehydrated! After the beating and scourging by the Romans, he had lost too much blood and sweat and, to top it off, the soldiers gave him a sponge soaked in vinegar wine when he said he was thirsty!"

"Your water-powered mutant theory still doesn't explain the Resurrection!" I say.

"I'll get back to you on that," she finishes, getting back to her melting Rocky Road.

Afterglow (based on a collaborative idea with Sonia Salazar)

The year was 2027. People were more disconnected than ever. Aside from all the technological gadgets at their disposal, a new pill had come on the market the year before called Orgazmo. Sexual partners were no longer necessary for an incredible release. Not only sex addicts or deviants, but "normal" everyday folk rushed to purchase this medical breakthrough. The secret government was thrilled as less money could be spent on diseases, etc. for their depopulation plans. But...pleasure always came with a price. Severe side effects began to emerge among the heavy users. Some had strokes; others heart attacks, while a few slipped into comas, never to awaken. And one...he became a homicidal maniac...this is his story.

Joseph

He got out of his old beat-up Ford Taurus, knees almost buckling. Only 45 and his joints hurt like a senior citizen's. It wasn't always this way. Just a few years ago, he had had the stamina and physique of a college man. That was before Monica left him. Before that whore had lain with her ex-husband, and drinking and other drugs had taken their toll on his mind and body. Until he discovered Orgazmo, that is. Everything had been euphoric for a little while. Like a street-legal morphine mixed with Viagra, but with a bonus handful of mind-blowing orgasms.

At least that's what it had been like for almost a full year. Then the headaches began, and then he couldn't reach orgasm, whether he used the pill or tried the old-fashioned selfie. Desperate for a release, but craving some revenge as well, Joseph had sought out his ex-girlfriend and killed her and her ex-husband as they lay naked in bed. And he had climaxed so much during that blood-fest that he'd had to change his pants and boxers after he got home. After jerking off again.

For the last few months, Joseph had turned that accidental discovery into a new hobby. He had sharpened up his father's old machete and started driving up into nearby woods, creeks, local and national parks. For a good explosive come, the victims had to be a couple and preferably, he had to take them while they were in the middle of a sexual act. Then, and only then, were his releases ensured. So much in fact, that he hacked them up while wearing Depends adult diapers.

Part of him worried about getting caught, perhaps not in the act, but after the fact. His method of operation was very 1980's slasher film cliché after all. Joseph was confident in several things. First and foremost, law enforcement hardly ventured into the places he chose. Second, he made a point of either burying, burning or otherwise disposing of his victims and third, he hadn't yet returned to the same scene of a crime.

Lisa and Juan

The middle-aged couple had been together for three years. In that time, she had got him to see why she loved the outdoors. Before her, Juan had been content to just sit at home and watch TV or read a good book. Once she shared her love of nature hikes and walks along the beach, his life was totally changed for the better.

Although Lisa was clearly the more sexually experienced of the two, Juan had gotten her to be a tad more adventurous. It had taken a while, but he persuaded her to let him go down on her on a fire road up in Azusa Canyon. They had tried on a hike before that, but were interrupted by some Chinese hikers walking by a little too closely.

Lisa never liked to plan much, not outings, let alone sex. But, much to Juan's delight, she had let hints drop that maybe, just maybe, she might be tempted to try something naughty near a creek somewhere. Their adult fun wasn't that frequent, as she was going thru menopause, and he suffered from occasional erectile dysfunction. But, when it did happen, they were both content. They felt a bit like rebels in that, not so much because they were older and still enjoying each other psychically, but most of their friends, even the married couples, were now using Orgazmo rather than old-fashioned carnal knowledge. Juan and Lisa agreed that while they could, they were going to continue what he called making love, and she still referred to as screwing. Physical acts would always be better than any drug; on that they wholeheartedly agreed.

So the couple had driven about 15 miles up Burro Canyon and parked at a rest stop, where they finished off the subway sandwiches and soda they had bought earlier that morning. The sun was already making its presence known, so Lisa suggested a hike along a path that ran parallel to a little creek that was shaded by pines and elm and other trees Juan couldn't name, but his lady could and often did.

An hour into the slightly strenuous walk, Juan pulled Lisa behind a strategically-placed boulder and started pawing her like a teenager, while kissing her neck and ears. Lisa didn't really get turned on by this foreplay, but she let him have his fun. His real skill was what he jokingly called his Australian kiss. Like a French kiss he said, but down under.

As he slid to his knees to undo her shorts, he began to undermine the mood by throwing in some un-needed commentary. "You know," Juan began, "instead of orgasm pills, pharmacies should invest in pills that would make you feel like that moment you first fall in love with a song…but you know, recreate it every time you hear that song or singer!"

"Oh shut up!" Lisa said half-jokingly. "Why do you have to talk anytime we're gonna fuck?"

Before Juan could answer, Lisa thrust her wildly overgrown pubes into his eager face, and he went to work while she moaned increasingly louder.

Joseph

Joseph had parked his Ford next to an equally beat-up Honda Accord. He steadied himself on that car, jerking his hand back from the scorching-hot hood. "Someone just got here!" he thought happily of possible new victims. Then, just as suddenly, he thought, "You dumb-fuck! The hood scalded your hand because it's high noon and hot as hell out here in the open! Yes, someone is out here, but we have to find them first, hope it's a couple and even better if they're rutting like filthy pigs!"

Joseph flipped a coin and began to walk south alongside the creek, following its peaceful gurgling downstream. His right hand felt at the machete, tucked tightly into a homemade leather sheath tied to his pants at the knee. The feel of his weapon rubbing against him was by itself giving him half a hard-on, so he forced his mind to think upon random things, such as "Dodgers baseball, the Stock Market Crash of 1929, that time his drunken aunt Rita let him feel her boobs when he was fifteen."

His attempts at conjuring non-sexual images sometimes backfired, so it was that he was sporting a full-sized erection by the time he came upon his prey. Joseph grinned like a madman as he pulled his machete free. There was no mistaking that sound. It was a woman in the throes of a powerful orgasm. "This couple had no need of a special pill," he thought enviously, crawling over a large rock to peer over.

Joseph was sweating profusely as he reached the top of the boulder. This was common before a kill, as his heart rate increased and the excitement reached its literal climax with the violent act to come.

He gazed hungrily at the scene of debauchery before him. Sure, he thought, that word generally meant sex, drugs and alcohol, but he could swear there was the hint of marijuana in the air and besides, he had passed several empty beer cans on his way here.

Something gave him pause though. The woman wasn't exceptionally attractive. Her breasts were average; she had a slight paunch to her belly, and apparently hadn't used a razor downstairs in years. Her mate didn't seem to mind as he lapped hungrily at her groin and inner thighs, as her moan diminished into a contented sort of whimpering.

No, it wasn't in her ordinary body, but her face. No the gorgeous brown eyes, nor the cute almost child-like dimples accentuating her chubby cheeks. It wasn't those facial traits, yet all of them combined. She was basking in…what was the word? Afterglow. And then Joseph's mind flashed back to Monica. After especially good sex, she would need a few minutes to collect herself, to just lay there, all sweat and smiles, glowing from a mutually pleasurable experience. That was before he killed her, before she cheated. When she had loved him, or said she did, and all they had needed was each other. Nobody else and no goddamn pills.

Joseph slid back off the boulder and trudged almost silently the way he had come. The murder spree was over just as suddenly as it had begun. It wasn't through some divine revelation, nor was he now a good, law-abiding citizen. No, it was simply the fact that Joseph realized he would no longer obtain sexual release from his vicious pastime. And what would be the point in murder if there were not some kind of reward after all?

Joseph mulled over his options. Turn himself in to the authorities? Absolutely not. He didn't feel enough guilt to spend the rest of his life in jail. Kill himself? Even less chance of hat since he had no real remorse and besides, he knew there was no more danger to the public, from him at the least.

One thing he knew for sure. As soon as he returned home, Joseph was discarding his supply of Orgazmo pills. From now on, he'd do it the old-fashioned way...cocaine and hookers. He chuckled softly as he reached his car. No, maybe, just maybe, he would try again. He would search for a real-life connection, another partner to share whatever life he had left to live. It would be difficult. It might bring its share of pain. But the reward would make it all worth it. He saw no other choice.

Author's Afterthought

"If I don't write to you anymore it's because I'm very tired and also because with me, as with you, there is nothing new to write about... In the End, as the Muslims: It is Written! That's Life and it's no laughing matter."

-Arthur Rimbaud
1882

Milton Keynes UK
Ingram Content Group UK Ltd.
UKHW012203150124
436080UK00003B/282

9 781478 789000